D0056381

Trophy
Son

Also by Douglas Brunt

Ghosts of Manhattan
The Means

Trophy
Son

Douglas Brunt

ST. MARTIN'S PRESS ❦ NEW YORK

This is a work of fiction. All of the characters, organizations, and events portrayed in this novel are either products of the author's imagination or are used fictitiously.

TROPHY SON. Copyright © 2017 by Douglas Brunt. All rights reserved. Printed in the United States of America. For information, address St. Martin's Press, 175 Fifth Avenue, New York, NY 10010.

www.stmartins.com

Designed by Steven Seighman

Library of Congress Cataloging-in-Publication Data

Names: Brunt, Douglas, author.
Title: Trophy son : a novel / Douglas Brunt.
Description: First Edition. | New York : St. Martin's Press, 2017.
Identifiers: LCCN 2017000907| ISBN 9781250114808 (hardback) |
    ISBN 9781250114815 (e-book)
Subjects: LCSH: Sports stories. | Domestic fiction. | BISAC: FICTION /
    Literary. | FICTION / Sports.
Classification: LCC PS3602.R868 T76 2017 | DDC 813/.6—dc23
LC record available at https://lccn.loc.gov/2017000907

Our books may be purchased in bulk for promotional, educational, or business use. Please contact your local bookseller or the Macmillan Corporate and Premium Sales Department at 1-800-221-7945, extension 5442, or by e-mail at MacmillanSpecialMarkets@macmillan.com.

First Edition: May 2017

10 9 8 7 6 5 4 3 2 1

once again for Megyn

PART I

I know I was born and I know that I'll die
The in between is mine

—Eddie Vedder

1

I n the end, man shapes the world, but the world gets the first crack at us. We're not much more than a puddle before we're two years old, and then more years to develop so we can survive on our own. Until then we take in more impressions than we give.

A tennis racket lurks in my earliest memories like a sick relative who had come to live with us. When I look at my baby pictures, there it is, resting in my crib in the place of a rattle or chew toy. I've talked to some players who say they know exactly the moment when their lives took the hard turn into professional tennis. It's when they first left home to live full time in a tennis academy or when they first put a coach on payroll or when they first took prize money and officially dropped amateur status.

I had no sensation of milestones and the power to value a moment was never granted to me. My parents had the plan for my life from the moment my mother tested positive with me. Looking back now, I'd say the hard turn for me was when I left school after the eighth grade to play tennis full time and study some with a travelling tutor.

At the time it didn't feel like a hard turn at all. I'd been told for several years that I'd be leaving school after the eighth grade so it had the reassurance of a promise kept. It was no different from waking up on any other day.

In the average day then, I'd spend seven hours on the court in our backyard in Radnor, Pennsylvania, with my dad blasting tennis balls at me from a machine. The rest of the day we'd talk tennis strategy, watch game film and train with weights.

In the winter we'd leave behind the Main Line suburbs and go rent a place in Florida with a tennis court so we could do the same year-round. Dad was a retired hedge fund manager who made enough millions to retire and focus on my game. Before that, he was on the 1984 US Olympic swimming team. No medals. He was accustomed to winning at everything but no medals in 1984.

By the time I was fourteen, I was good enough to beat the crap out of a decent college player so every few weeks we'd travel to a college where nobody knew me but that Dad had scouted out.

Once we drove down to the courts at the University of Pennsylvania. Dad said, "Get ready to fight, Anton." We're Greek. Dad loved being Greek. Ancient warrior-athletes.

For the tenth time, he told me how to approach the court, taunt the players on the college team, bait them into a match, bait them into putting money on the line. He said to me on this trip as he did on every trip, "A friendly game will ruin you. Play with adversity, with animosity. No friendly games."

I realized this also meant no friends, at least not anywhere near tennis. Tennis is about only hate and suffering.

What Dad saw in me that he didn't see in my brother Panos was that I could handle the hate. I could suffer. I could take the hate, give some back then take some more. With my brother, the fight would fall out of him. After a while, he'd flip Dad the bird and walk off the court. When Dad saw his absolute mental dominance over my brother was slipping, his efforts turned abusive and physical. I was on my brother's side but I'm a people pleaser on some level and I wanted a different result and knew how to get it. I stayed on the court.

I took the punishment and by twelve I had used it to become an elite junior player. By fourteen, I was on the Penn campus to humiliate a Division I college player.

Late February is early in the tennis season. It was warm on a Sunday, and the first warm days make you notice for the first time in months that the branches are naked. I would look at the trees and try to imagine them with their leaves back on. Dad knew the team did informal hitting at 2pm and would be on the outdoor courts. I carried my biggest and most ridiculous-looking tennis bag and wore a pristine, white tennis outfit.

Dad said, "Don't be a little cocky. Be massively cocky. Humble and confident seems real. You need to blow so hard they don't believe a word you're saying. And you need to piss them off. Make them crave a match to take you down."

We parked far from the courts. Dad put five one-hundred-dollar bills in my pocket, then we split up. He walked to a place where he could watch the play without being seen, partly to watch the match and partly to be there to save me if a fight broke out. Dad was 6'4". His swimming weight was two hundred pounds, but at this time he was two-forty and mostly muscle. He loved asserting his bigness. He had black hair, olive skin and looked old-country Greek, tough and dangerous.

I saw a couple college kids hitting on the courts and four others sitting on a bench nearby in sweat clothes with racket bags. They looked like nice guys. I would have preferred to say hi, talk with them, hear what school and a normal life can be like, laugh about something. But Dad had taught me that this kind of average life was wasteful, slothful, damaging to a life of excellence. These boys were a breed to be pitied, observed only, like species in a zoo. Do not touch the glass, do not feed the animals.

Anyway, I had a job to do here. Dad had given me a few opening lines.

There were eight guys, all dressed in similar sweat clothes. Some were hitting, most were lounging on courtside benches like actors backstage after the play. I sat down as loud as I could on the bench next to them and said, "Hi, kids."

They looked at me and smiled. Later I grew to be 6'3" and strong but then I was 5'10" and a rail with the flat, invisible muscles that active, early teens have. They didn't say anything.

The grass lawns around the courts were thin and wilted, just starting to come back to life. A squirrel back on his haunches looked up at us from his nut which he held with both arms like a mixing bowl of brownie batter. Remnants of leaves from the fall, rotted to small pieces by the long winter, blew in wisps at the bases of trees and in small piles and soon would return to dust.

I pointed at one of the guys hitting balls on the court. "What a joke that guy is."

They stopped talking with each other and looked at me.

I said, "I must be in the wrong place. Is this U Penn? I thought this was U Penn."

"It's U Penn," one of them said.

"Well, who the hell are you guys? Where's the tennis team?" I said.

They looked at each other. "We're the tennis team."

I did my best to look shocked, shocked. "Bullshit." I pointed to the court again. "You can't tell me that guy plays on a tennis team. Maybe an elementary school team."

One of them said, "He plays number two singles."

They found me insulting but also funny. Another of them laughed and said, "Nice tennis whites. Beat it, you little punk."

I said, "If this is the quality of tennis at U Penn, then you can beat this," and I stroked the handle of my tennis racket. That was improvised and I felt good about it. "Obviously I can't get a decent match around here. Where's Nadal when you need him. Andy Murray."

One said, "I think there's a middle school down the street. Go look for a match there."

I said, "Middle school. That's funny. Listen, if you don't want to play me just for the instructional benefit to you, then play me for money."

"How much money?"

I said, "Five hundred." I pulled out the five bills from my pocket. This is the hard part. You can sound as ridiculous as you like, but money makes it real.

They were stunned. Nobody took the bet yet. I said, "Is this U Penn or U Pussy?" Dad scripted this stuff and he thought this last line was a gem. It worked. There had already been too much shit-talking and ego involved for it not to work.

The guys on the court had walked over by then to listen. "Who wants to play the kid?"

"I'll play him," said the number two singles player who had been hitting.

"Where's your five hundred bucks?" I said.

Together they had two-fifty so we all waited while one kid ran to the ATM. The courts were a small oasis in Penn's urban campus and a deli with an ATM was only a thousand feet away. I started hitting rallies with the number two singles player whose name was Jim. I said, "You're okay, Jim. You look a little better from out here on the court than you did from the bench. You have a heavy ball."

It was a clear day, sunny, no breeze. It was about fifty degrees out which is great tennis weather once you get moving. A commercial jet flew overhead, low enough that the sound echoed across the sky so you couldn't sense where the noise was from.

"You're damn right, squirt," he said.

I wasn't hitting my best stuff yet. I'd just get loose for a while before we played the match.

My hand-eye coordination has always been great. Great baseball hitters can write a number on a baseball with Magic Marker and when it comes at them at ninety miles per hour they can read the number. I've never tried that but I bet I can do it. Things move to me slower and I get there faster. Take that gift and work it out on a tennis court for seven hours a day and you get me. When the match started I knew I'd shift my game to the next gear and put a beating on Jim that he'd be dying to tell his friends about in a few years every time he'd see me on national television.

I just wished I didn't need to be such a jerk about it. I didn't know it then but I resented Dad for making me do this with people. I wasn't able to name it as resentment, but that's what it was. Dad never let anyone come to like me. I was trapped in his boot camp, developing an edge that no other fourteen-year-old could match.

There is no question it gave me toughness, a knowledge that no opponent across the net could fathom my training, but it was all built on hate.

We had rallied for ten minutes when the kid returned with the money. We put all the cash in an empty tennis ball can. They made jokes about having their drinking money for the night.

A guy about fifty years old in sweat clothes had taken a seat in the bleachers. I thought he was probably the coach. I didn't see Dad but I knew he was there. I knew he was smiling like a hunter with a doe in his crosshairs.

Jim graciously let me serve first without spinning for it.

I got to my spot on the baseline and said, "These are good."

"No practice serves?" said Jim.

"No."

Jim shrugged. It was his last relaxed gesture.

At fourteen, I could already serve a hundred miles per hour. More impressive than the speed was that my service form was perfect. It was beautiful, and I could place the ball anywhere I wanted. Anyone watching knew that with a few years and a few inches I'd be serving one-forty.

I uncorked an ace up the middle. It landed an inch inside the T. Jim didn't move. His knees flinched to the middle but his feet never moved.

I looked to the bench. It was a Susan Boyle moment. Shock and awe. There was no apparent correlation between the performance and the package. Other than the team, the coach and my hidden father, there was no one around to see my quiet victory. The coach was already walking down from the bleachers like Simon Cowell ready to offer me a recording deal except this guy was no billionaire and I had no interest in a college scholarship. I knew I'd never go to college. I didn't even go to the ninth grade for Christ's sake.

If poor Jim had harbored any hope of playing pro tennis, it died that afternoon. He realized there was another class of player out there and he couldn't handle the fourteen-year-old version of it.

Jim had a steady game with few errors but his ball had no pop. He couldn't push anyone around. He would just hang around and make his opponent beat him but his ball set up exactly the way I liked it. I got to balls early, stepped into my shot and ripped my swing as hard as I could. When I was older I'd hit harder, but that day was the hardest I'd ever hit in a match to that point.

I beat Jim 6-0, 6-1. I gave him a game in the second set because I'm not as ruthless as Dad and the goodness I felt from doing it meant more than the criticism I would get for it on the ride home.

They were all so amazed by the severity of the beating that they forgot to feel hustled. They handed me the can of cash and gave me some pats on the back. They were sure they'd watch me win matches at the US Open in a few years.

The coach walked over to talk with me. I glanced up and saw Dad sitting in the bleachers. He'd come out of hiding and looked relaxed. He didn't care about the money, but he did need to make sure I didn't get hurt.

The coach smiled at me and said, "What's your name, son?"

"Anton."

"How old are you Anton?"

"Fourteen."

"Where do you play?"

"Mostly my backyard. Some satellite tournaments." I knew he was about to praise me and I was excited to hear it. Dad never praised me.

The coach looked around and saw Dad and knew exactly. Then the coach surprised me. "I don't expect to see you around here again. Ever. I don't like hustlers. Get going now."

I picked up my massive tennis bag and started for the bleachers.

Then the coach said, "Anton," and he walked over to me, still out of earshot of Dad. He put a hand on my shoulder and looked nice again. "Balance."

"Balance?"

He said, "Don't think about what I'm saying all at once now. But every once in a while, when you have a decision to make, think about balance."

"Okay."

"Good luck," he said.

2

Dad met Mom in 1983 during the lead up to the 1984 games. She was an Olympic downhill skier. In those days, the winter and summer games were held in different cities but in the same year so there was more intermingling of winter and summer athletes at social functions.

Mom was a much less intense person than Dad, but a natural athlete who loved skiing. She was 5'7" with strong legs and a low center of gravity. She didn't medal either, but she became well known in America for how attractive she was. Certainly she became known to Dad.

In the 80s she kept her long blonde hair in a ponytail that would whip around from under her ski helmet when she came down the mountain. After kids she cut it shoulder length.

The awards of their athletic careers filled our attic. I'd go up there once in a while to poke around old pictures of them in their teenage years and wonder what kind of people they were then.

There were huge trophies and photos of them competing or waving from the winners' podium and the pictures were all beautifully framed with a caption to identify the event, but they all sat in boxes like a travelling museum exhibit that never got unpacked.

It was a long time before I realized that all this stuff made Dad more angry because there wasn't an Olympic medal with it. The more grand everything was, the more apparent that something was missing.

Dad was a sprinter. His best event was the 100-meter freestyle and he was expected to medal in 1984. In the final he was in the lane next to an Australian who was also a favorite to medal. You can see in the old TV footage that as they were stepping on the platform by the pool, the Australian said something to Dad, then Dad said something back and pointed a finger at the guy.

Dad never said what the words were. He shrugged it off as nothing but the Australian had gotten in his head and Dad was late off the platform. There's no way to make that up in a 100-meter race. Dad came in sixth. At least another American took the gold that year.

We drove back from U Penn with Dad laughing and talking about points in the match the whole way. He scolded me about giving away a game, but lightly. He let me keep the five hundred bucks but we had to go deposit it in the bank. Five hundred bucks can buy a lot of distraction from tennis.

We pulled into our driveway and I walked into the living room. Sparely furnished. Area rugs that left lots of hardwood uncovered, piano, a few paintings on the wall but mostly white space, all like it was done by a staging company in preparation for a real estate sale. My older brother, Panos, was at the dining room table with his homework spread out in front of him. Greek. Dark hair, dark skin, a thin and less dangerous-looking version of Dad.

"How'd it go?" said Panos to me.

"Okay," I said.

"Great," said Dad. "Total annihilation."

Panos looked from Dad back to me. Panos would have liked to be a better tennis player and therefore get some admiration from Dad, even attention. But he knew that's not how it worked around here. He was mostly relieved that Dad's focus wasn't on him. He also felt guilty that he'd abandoned me to Dad's obsessive behavior. Panos had plenty of his own stuff to work out for a young kid, always sipping on a cocktail of jealousy, relief and guilt.

Panos said, "Dad, why do you make him go do that stuff? It's sick."

"Shut up, Panos. You're not a competitor. Don't talk about things you don't understand." Then Dad went upstairs.

Panos and I exchanged looks. I appreciated his effort to help, though now I felt guilty that Dad lashed at him for trying to help me. That sort of thing happened all the time. Every family has its dysfunction. This was the Stratis form of it.

Panos said, "Want to get out of here? Go see a movie?"

Panos was three years older and a senior at the high school where I would be if I were still in school. He was lucky to be there. When I was in the seventh grade I played a coed softball game for fun. Dad had made it clear I was never to play anything but tennis, but this was just a one-time goofy thing with the girls. I turned my ankle rounding first base. When Dad got the call he drove right to school and went to the middle school athletic director. Dad shouted at the guy and when the guy made the mistake of shouting back, Dad put him in the wall. It turned into a big deal at the time but the school didn't mess with me or Panos. "Sure," I said. "I'll take a quick shower and change."

Twelve steps to the second floor. Turn right and it was three steps more to my bedroom door. There were sixty-two and one-third tiles on the floor of the shower stall if you include all the tiles that I approximated were cut either in half or in thirds to fit the space of the stall. I showered for one hundred seconds unless it was right after a match in which case I showered for five hundred seconds. I counted this in my head and I counted a perfect second. I tested myself against a clock almost every day.

I noticed the smallest shit everywhere I went. A little piece of garbage, a car in a parking lot with headlights on, all the words on all the signs, how many steps it was from anywhere to anywhere else. But if I ever got interrupted, it didn't matter. I didn't need to have the count. I didn't need to see everything around me, I was just observing. Looking for new information.

It's funny to think of now. I had all the OCD symptoms but I wasn't OCD then and I'm not today. I practiced OCD just to fill a void.

When I look back at these teenage years, it's one thing to do rote recounting of events and another to penetrate to the contemporaneous emotions. I was a stressed-out, anxious kid and only with the benefit of hindsight can I link the stress to the source.

I could never make the link then. At the time I just figured I was OCD, and that actually stressed me out too. But the real problem was that I just had no stimulation. At least no stimulation I wanted. No birthday parties, no dates with girls to be nervous and excited about, no new experiences. I ate, slept, played tennis and rested for more tennis. When I rested I didn't want to think about tennis but had nothing else to think about so I counted and noticed things around me. My brain had to do something and that was all the material it had to work with.

Panos knew it was better to slip out. Let Dad think Panos was studying and I was resting. He'd hear the car start but by that time it would be too late. We could be down the road and pretend we didn't hear our cell phones ring.

These were the oasis moments of my teenage years and worthwhile even if Dad was pissed when we got home. Panos and I jogged to the car with stomach muscles clenched and barely breathing. Panos drove a Porsche 911 that cost Dad less than my tennis travel each year so it was a way to balance things out between the kids. We laughed when we got on the street, turned the radio way up and I looked at the front lawns of other people's lives.

Dad landscaped the perimeter of our tennis court with dense, twelve-foot-high hedges so that we couldn't see the neighbors or even our own house when playing. There was a path of flagstones leading from our house through two acres of lawn down a slope to the court. Forty-three flagstones. I would step past the double overhead hedges to the court that held back the outside world so that I felt like I was boarding a ship at sea.

"Forehands down the line," he said and he angled the ball machine toward my deuce court. On this particular day I was nine years old. Still early in my training with Dad, still figuring out my limits. It was more than ninety degrees in August. Dad liked to train at the hottest time of day to condition me for adversity.

The machine pumped balls to me in three-second intervals. I hit fifty while he would retrieve them and dump them back in the machine to maintain a never-ending inventory of practice balls.

"Cross court," he yelled, and I adjusted to pull my forehands across my body for fifty more balls.

We did backhands down the line, then cross court, then he changed the setting on the machine so that it would oscillate like a fan and move me around.

I could feel the direct sun going through layers of skin like I was being microwaved, but worse and closer was the heat radiating up from our baked hard court. I had drenched my clothes with sweat, my temples were pounding and my feet inside my sneakers were the hottest of all. I could feel the unnatural temperature. "Water break," I said, my voice high, far from pubescent.

"No water break. This is a match."

"I drink water during matches."

"You want to be ready for a match, you train for more than a match."

"I need water."

"Fifty more, then water."

The pounding in my temples was no longer a beat but a constant hum and I felt a surge of energy as my anger grew. Boys at that age are ill-equipped to manage anger so it usually gets energetic and confused and crosses into rage.

I started hitting my hardest shots. I wasn't thinking about form or footwork or keeping the ball in the court at all. I just wanted power and I directed the balls at the machine, and at Dad. Balls were reaching him on the fly like comets and he had to skip out of the way.

"Watch it, Anton."

I started hitting my normal forehands again. The machine drummed away while he collected balls along the back fence with his back to me. With no calculation of consequence I cranked a forehand toward the back fence and Dad. With the experience of hundreds of thousands of hits, my mind could instinctively compute the flight path of a ball and I sensed danger. This screaming line drive made right for the back of his head like a sniper shot. I stood frozen in terrified amazement and listened for the hollow pop of tennis ball on hard skull. The impact knocked his head forward. He turned to me with a disbelieving face.

"Water break," I said, ignoring the calamity. I walked to the net post where we kept the cooler. I'd had a few sips before he took his first steps toward me. I knew it would be bad so I drank what I could before he reached me.

He grabbed the water from my hand and threw it over the hedges in a motion that was spasmodic with anger. He kept his voice weirdly even as though if he could control his voice he could control me. "Get back on the baseline."

"I need a break. I'm getting tired and playing sloppy. I don't want to practice sloppy."

"Get back on the baseline." This time with an even voice but through gritted teeth.

"Two minutes break," I said.

He turned from me ninety degrees for a moment and when he turned back his face had reddened and contorted into a berserk version of my father with fury and force, the kind of power that gives humans the desperate and inhuman strength to lift a car or break a wall. In a voice like a passing express train he yelled, "Get back on the baseline."

So I did. In a typical practice a player might hit a thousand balls. In ninety-plus degrees, that's a good practice. Before the yell, I'd hit five hundred. I hit five hundred more after the yell and the length of my baseline was a puddle of my own sweat. I lay down

my racket and started to take off my shirt which had long ago ab-
sorbed the maximum of sweat.

"Put your shirt back on."

"Dad, it weighs ten pounds."

"Put it on. You're match training. You don't play topless tournaments."

"I don't play tournaments like this either. I'd change shirts. At
least let me put on a dry shirt."

Reasonable. But he'd already issued a command and that mattered more than reason. He wouldn't change commands on my
suggestion. "Keep that shirt on." The ball machine pumped balls
down my backhand side.

"Jesus," I said under my breath and I stood, enjoying a few moments not shuffling my feet into position and ripping ground strokes.
Four more balls passed. Twelve seconds.

"You're wasting my time and yours," he said. "You have three
more balls to get that shirt back on and play."

"Dad." Futile protest.

"One," he said. Three seconds later, "Two."

"Dad."

"Three," and he started walking to my side of the court in the
same deliberate and resolute way he'd done earlier.

I fanned the shirt out and started my arms through. It was hard
to pull over me because it was so wet. I saw the facial tics as his
inner berserker wrestled into control. I got my head through the
collar right as he squared up in front of me. That just gave him
something to grab on to.

At that age I weighed about ninety pounds, just more than a
third of Dad. He took two fists full of shirt and jerked me off the
ground above his head and walked me back against the court fence

and leaned into me, making the fence bow out, keeping eye contact the whole way.

From my earliest years he wouldn't tolerate slacking off, complaints, and certainly not talking back. No kid stuff whatsoever. My fits of youth were broken as he would break a racehorse. When I felt my own rage, he wouldn't allow the expression of it.

"You keep that goddamn shirt on and play. I am sick and tired of you not listening. I swear to God, Anton, if you waste one more second of my time out here I will smack you." All the while he pushed me deeper into the fence and I felt the diamond shapes of the wire digging into my skin.

"Okay," I managed, terrified. For the first time scared of a real beating.

He put me down and we played on. Five hundred more balls which was of course too much, too long to be out there, but I realized later that he felt some guilt at having been so physical with me and wanted to put time between that moment and when he next spoke to me.

At the end of the five hundred balls he said, "Okay, come on up, let's get some water."

We met halfway at the net where I drank water fast, so my stomach hurt. He put his arm around my shoulders and pulled my little body into his mass. "You're one hell of a player," he said. We were both sweaty messes. "One hell of a player." He kissed the top of my head. Then he knelt down in front of me and held my face in both his hands. "You have a great attitude and you're working hard and I'm going to be there with you the whole way. You're going to be one of the truly great players and I love you very much."

Our training got more and more that way. Beat me, love me. Like Ike Turner.

Dad had been both my trainer and coach from the beginning. He had done the same for Panos who was slightly smaller and less physical than I was. Panos grew to be 6'1", two inches shorter than I would be, but he was quick and could have been a great player. The problem was that Dad made what he thought were mistakes in the way that he disciplined Panos and he wouldn't make those mistakes with me. He had been inconsistent with Panos, let him have too many glimpses of life not under Dad's thumb. He made sure early on with me.

Mom and Dad always let me read. They encouraged it. If I couldn't go anywhere physically, I could at least take a journey with a book. When I read a book I liked, I would then read everything else by that author so my reading came in phases defined by the writer. I had a Hemingway phase, Faulkner, John Irving, Nelson DeMille. When I was fourteen, I was in the middle of my Dickens phase.

I loved Dickens. Unfairness, unhappiness, suffering, heroes and villains, glimmers of hope at love and of a way out. *David Copperfield* was the best and the best of that was the opening line, the idea of being the hero of your own life. I thought so much back then about whether or not I would be the hero of my own life. Now I understand how turned around my interpretation of that line was. Back then I took it as a mandate to succeed, win tournaments, be the best. But being the number one tennis player doesn't make me the hero of my own life. It makes me the hero of someone else's life. Maybe Dad's.

Being the hero of my own life is about something else, something internal. It's about who has their hands on the steering wheel that's inside me. It needed to be me and it never was then, and I didn't understand that until much later.

At fourteen I equated heroism with winning at tennis. I was determined and successful.

Dad wanted to manage me the way Richard Williams managed Venus and Serena. He wanted to develop me in secret, apart from the tennis tour, then I would be this enigma who one day sprang onto the circuit and kicked everyone's ass.

But men develop differently than women. Female prodigies can dominate the pros as early as fifteen. Men take several more years to mature physically and I think mentally too. There was no way to keep me in secret that long. I needed to improve by playing matches with good players. That meant playing satellite tournaments. I started to win. A lot. I got noticed.

I was not yet fifteen and won a competitive sixteen-and-under tournament in Florida. I was playing great then, and I was happy. Not because of my tennis results but because of the life of travel. Travel was new to me and new stuff made me happy. I hadn't learned to hate hotels yet. The palm trees, flat terrain and big skies of Florida still felt exotic and were a pleasant benefit of my hard work.

Dad and I would sit in first class where I'd look through magazine pages of impossibly blue waters, white sand and tan legs. Pictures of healthy indulgences that were restorative and deserved. Achievement and reward. Those places were never our destination but I loved those magazines and studied them.

"Anton!"

"Yes?"

"I'm with USTA Magazine."

"Hi." I was walking off the court after the quick ceremony at the net for my tournament win. Dad saw us from the bleachers but the reporter got to me first.

"May I ask you some questions?"

"Sure," I said.

"What will you do after winning a match like this?"

"Take a shower. Eat something." My answer was so moronic I realized it may even have sounded flip. "I think Dad and I are flying home to Philadelphia tonight." This sounded more sophisticated.

The reporter held up a recording device. "Which pro do you admire most, past or present?"

I thought Agassi, Rafter, McEnroe, Federer. My game wasn't much like any of theirs, I just liked them. My game was more like Marat Safin. Tall guy, big serve, moved well, ugly but good two-handed backhand. I was trying to pick one of my favorites when Dad stepped up to us and said, "Anton's not like anyone else. He's a unique talent."

The reporter said, "You must be Mr. Stratis. Congratulations on your son's win today."

"Thank you."

"I'm with USTA Magazine. I'm hoping to ask a few questions for an article we'd like to run on Anton."

Dad wanted to say no. Every blood vessel in his body was pumping no but the interview was already somewhat under way which meant he'd have to cut it off right in the guy's face and that could result in bad publicity. All he wanted was no publicity for me.

I had not been expected to go far in this tournament, let alone win it, so Dad was in as great a mood as I'd ever seen him and this carried the moment. "Sure," he said. "Five minutes."

Back then, in conversations I always stood with my head tipped down a bit and I'd look ahead at the other person the way people look over reading glasses that are perched on the bridge of their nose.

It wasn't that I was shy. It was that I was handsome and I'd never gotten anything but scorn from Dad for being handsome. It's one thing not to emphasize positive feedback on looks. It's another to actively de-emphasize it.

Dad knew attention to looks diluted attention to tennis. Not just the potential distraction of girls, but he didn't want me to have anything of personal value other than skill on the court. He'd prefer me ugly. Obedient and focused like a dog.

The next month my tutor came over to the house—a retired history teacher from the Philadelphia public school system. He was old and smelled old. He talked slow and was boring as hell, and even then I knew this was a deliberate choice by Dad to head off any interest in academics that might have developed. But he was a nice, gentle guy and I liked him. His name was Ned. Boring.

I was so ready to love academics that Ned's dryness didn't matter much. We'd share reading lists and talk about books and the characters in them. All in all, we would have a nice time together.

Mom would check in on the lessons sometimes. She wanted to be there and be a part of it but didn't know how. I could see her look of uncertainty when she'd open the door a quarter of the way to ask in a bright voice how we were doing, then her awkward expression during the expectant silence after our answer of just fine, then she'd step back and close the door like releasing a tent flap she'd been peeking through.

Ned was an avid tennis fan, though he admitted he was never much of a player himself. When we'd get together he'd ask about my last matches and my training and what I thought about the top pros. He'd come watch any of my matches that were local. He liked to follow my embryonic tennis career in a way that I appreciated.

"Good morning, Anton." We sat across from each other in the dining room at a long rectangular table for twelve and we'd huddle in one corner by the sideboard table with the silver service tray on top.

"Hi, Ned." I'd guess he was about seventy. His name was Mr. Billings but he insisted I call him Ned. I think he hated being called Mr. Billings all those years of teaching.

"I was excited to see this." He pulled a copy of *USTA Magazine* from his leather messenger bag then slid it across the table to me. It was opened to the article on me and there was a picture of my face that took a third of one page. "Congratulations."

I hadn't seen it. We didn't subscribe to *USTA Magazine,* or if we did, Dad didn't let me see it. I was sure Dad wouldn't want me to see this. I leaned over it. The words were all blurry because my eyes were focused on the photo.

It was a nice picture of me. I was looking right into the camera, my smile didn't look forced. It looked as though I might be happy and unafraid. More than that, it was just me in the photo. Not me and Dad. A person who saw this photo and read this article might think, Here's this impressive kid, doing it, making it happen.

I'd never thought of myself that way. Not really. I was always just doing what I was supposed to do, what I was told, which was always made very clear to me. I'd always thought of myself as carrying out instructions as though I were an appendage to someone else's body.

This article made me feel like an independent force. There was no mention of Dad anywhere.

"Thank you," I said to Ned.

"You really smoked them at that tournament."

"I hope I can keep it up. That was the best I can play." A lot of the kids I played were almost two years older but the toughest match came against a kid who was only six months older. Ben Archer. I already knew I'd be seeing a lot more of Ben Archer.

"You'll get better and better," said Ned. "You're on the earliest part of the curve. It isn't even steep yet." Ned smiled. "Let's start with some calculus."

The only subject I liked was literature. I hated calculus but I liked my time with Ned. He was kind and treated me like a whole person, and it was something else to do.

Two weeks later I was at another satellite tournament in North Carolina. These are played at tennis centers, pretty small venues, not like the big stadiums you see on TV for the majors. From watching professional matches as a kid, I always had thought there'd be something of scale, something big, but there wasn't. It was flat and sprawling. Aluminum bleachers by the courts, no buildings higher than two stories, nothing as big as a high school gym. The spectators usually had a professional connection to tennis or a family connection to a player or they just lived in the neighborhood down the street and thought it would make a fun afternoon to watch some decent tennis live. In North Carolina the tournaments offered sweet tea in an oversized thermos, a nice touch.

Security wasn't a big deal at these things so players and spectators wandered the grounds intermingled. There were never paparazzi of any kind. My brush with the reporter at the last tournament had been my first ever.

Dad walked with me to the court entrance for my first-round match. It was sixty-five degrees, sunny, slight breeze, and the calm of the day matched the calm of the people milling around us. Everything felt pleasant.

The match schedule was published in advance. Two reporters with cameras were by the court entrance and stepped forward as Dad and I approached. They waved, smiled and raised cameras to take a few shots.

Dad went nuts, chopping at cameras with his hands and yelling, "Get the fuck out of here."

Everyone was surprised by the suddenness and the sickness of his actions. I was surprised only by the suddenness. He must have harbored pent-up rage over the *USTA Magazine* article that he'd been given a chance to stop and didn't.

Dad had a long wingspan and when he swung his arms like that he seemed even bigger, like an angry bear. As soon as the reporters came to their senses, they ran like hell. There were a couple of volunteer ushers nearby but no security and the whole thing was finished in five seconds. Once the reporters ran, the people near us watched Dad and me walk on the court like nothing happened.

Dad stopped two steps into the court. He wasn't supposed to come on with me. "Focus, Anton. This is another test."

"Okay."

"Play great."

"I will."

I walked to the chair at the side of the court by the net and sat down. Alone. For the next couple hours I'd be in a bubble. That's where real tennis happens. All alone in a bubble.

That's the thing about tennis. There's no teammate to talk over strategy. There's no opponent near enough for a verbal exchange. I'm not even allowed to talk to a coach. It's isolation. In baseball a hitter's alone at the plate, a pitcher's alone on the mound. In basketball a player is alone on the free-throw line. But those are only moments. A moment later, the baseball players are back in the dugout slapping asses and spitting tobacco. The basketball player starts running the floor again with nine other guys. Even a boxer gets to rub foreheads and talk trash. My isolation is complete. Only swimming's isolation can compare to that of tennis.

Liz Betterton had asked me to a school dance. I would have been a sophomore at the time if I had stayed in school. I remembered her vividly from my eighth-grade year. She was one of the girls who developed early. Athletic curves and a full chest, long blonde hair sort of feathered the way Farrah Fawcett wore hers in the 1970s. She looked like someone's sexy older sister but was our age.

I had gone straight from the courts of a tournament match to a celebration dinner with Dad at the Wayne Hotel, a fancy boutique hotel near our home. White tablecloths, waiters dressed in white jackets and ties, which is rare for suburban Main Line. It was a small dining room with soft electrical lighting and candles and it was understood that for diners already seated it was not rude to pause conversation and observe new arrivals because that was worthy reconnaissance. Liz was there with her family.

She seemed to piece together who I was, the odd tennis prodigy who dropped out of school. She waved and I waved back, then we both got shy, though her shyness may have been only for effect.

Two days later she invited me to the dance and I went tuxedo shopping with Mom who was almost as excited as I was.

For every boy in my grade throughout middle school, Liz Betterton was an unattainable, celebrity crush. We'd all have hung posters of her in our lockers and on bedroom walls if posters of her existed. As it was we clicked, open-mouthed, at photos on her Facebook page.

Now I was dating her, kissing her, going places with her, talking on the phone for an hour at a time. Dad didn't like this. I knew because he pulled me aside and said exactly, "I don't like this, Anton. You're distracted."

This was the one area where Mom dug in and protected me. She would say, "Let them be, Dear," and she'd put her hands on her hips and look right at him. It was a look that said I've never fought you but on this I will and I'll find the strength to win. Dad liked his perfect record. He didn't want to set a precedent of losing a battle to Mom so he never engaged. He notionally allowed the relationship but set little skirmishes to interfere with me and Liz. He'd schedule practice sessions for late on a Saturday or enter me in a tournament to overlap a concert or event Liz and I had planned to attend.

His interference united Liz and me as rebels against the Empire. He took our romance and made it more adventurous, dangerous, Shakespearean.

It was still my first year with a driver's license. Panos let me borrow his car to pick up Liz and take her out. I pulled up in front of her house and the front door opened and she jogged out wearing a miniskirt and cowboy boots. She had a tiny purse on a spaghetti strap that crossed her chest, parting her breasts. The miniskirt flapped with her strides like a matador's red capote.

It was part of our routine never to go to the front door of either's house. It wasn't a social call. We were the rebels escaping parental clutches. There may as well have been a ladder down from a second-floor bedroom window.

She ducked, coming through the passenger door headfirst to kiss me and said, "Hi, Lover."

That was the best. Calling me Lover. I felt like a grown man. This gorgeous woman sat next to me and I put the car in drive.

"Panos did some shopping for us," I said.

"That sounds lovely."

Lovely, she said. I was living out a movie plot. I had no other social life to dilute this, so everything felt like a movie plot. "There's a picnic basket in the trunk he put together." It was an eighty-degree day in late June, warm breezes and birds chirping still felt new.

"Some wine, I hope."

"Of course."

"Good. All I want to do right now is stretch out against your long body and sip wine. Your dad won't come looking for you, will he?"

"No, no way."

"What if he did, and found you with me and a bottle of wine?"

She liked to imagine these confrontations, talk them through. I liked it too. It heightened the risk and in the role play we could insert ourselves as the heroic defenders of youth and romance and make ourselves more attractive to each other.

We drove to the Willows which is a beautiful park in Wayne that used to be a private estate. It's full of rolling grassy hills, old trees, ponds and also many geese so the trick is to find an area with no goose crap.

I found a spot for our blanket then devastated the wine cork, finally having to push the half-shredded thing back down into the bottle so we could drink, and I was feeling amateurish and undeserving of the name Lover.

She drank the wine and kissed my neck, then pushed me down and sat on my stomach. My hands instinctively went inside her miniskirt and grabbed the flesh of her ass with no panty to buffer my palms.

"I hope he does come. Asshole."

"Who?"

"Your dad."

"Oh," I said. "I'm not really hoping for that." I squeezed her ass. I had big hands and had a firm hold on her like a suction cup. She allowed it and seemed to like it.

"You're such a good athlete, baby. The way your body moves when you're out there. It's like you can do anything, like you're magic. And then your dad browbeats you and runs you down. Makes it ugly."

It was nice to have someone express outrage on my behalf. It calmed my own outrage even though it was also a validation. "Well, that's his way," I said, surprising myself, even as I uttered the words, that I made any defense of him.

"Then it's an awful way." She leaned forward and kissed me then said, "Roll over. I'm going to massage you."

We were in a remote part of the park. One other couple was a hundred yards away playing with their baby. I obeyed. We hadn't had sex of any kind in our four months together. We'd played around in underwear before, but that was it. She worked her fingers over my shoulders and lower back while I pointed my erection to the side so it had a place to go though it still raged against the weight of me on top of it.

Then Liz said these magical words to me and my erection. "Roll over again."

She lay down beside me and pulled a corner of the blanket up over our legs and hips. I had loose athletic shorts on which were easily shifted to let me out. She took me in her right hand.

Of course I had taken myself in my own hand before and done just fine, but there was something about the first touch of another. The first in my life. Her grasp of me sent a pulse through my body that arched my back and pointed my toes and was better than any orgasm I'd had prior to that time.

She kissed my ear and stroked my erection while I alternately stared at the sky and clenched my eyes shut.

In less than a minute I had come. She wiped me and herself with the blanket then poured us more wine while I lay back feeling that my time on Earth had been good.

We lay together, certain we were more wise than our adult tormentors, confident in the righteousness of our rebellion, smug about it, even.

My feelings for her were more powerful having overcome the adversity and isolation of my home. She was also my only escape, my only window into the real world, and the only competition that had ever tested Dad. "I love you," I said. I thought I did. No question I needed her and loved the thought of her.

She squeezed my neck and kissed me.

CHAPTER

6

I started losing. Bad, first-round losses that I couldn't explain. I didn't think the losing had anything to do with Liz. I didn't think it then and don't now. From today's perspective I'd say I was confused, unhappy and mentally spent when I'd step on the court so I had no mental toughness left for the match. I was emotionally exhausted. But at that time I had no understanding of what was happening to me. I had no answer for the question of why I was losing.

For most people, a kid losing some sporting events is the regular hard knocks that is a healthy part of growing up. But my whole world was so small. The only thing of value was winning at tennis and losing was Armageddon. Losing was real trauma for me.

And then there was Dad. He was more invested in tennis than I was. A loss to an inferior player would not be tolerated. If putting a physical beating on me would have helped, he'd have done it. With pleasure.

In Atlanta I lost first round to a player I should have toyed with. We drove back to the hotel in total silence. Eerie silence. We almost always stayed in a Marriott and these were the same damn hotel anywhere in the country, just as much as the McDonald's Quarter Pounder is the same burger anywhere. Between the hotel and the courts in any town there is nothing but sameness, but I've been to Atlanta many times in my career and it was a town especially devoid of personality. Everything with charm was burned to the ground during the Civil War, then everything was paved and rebuilt in a hurry. What I remembered of Atlanta was that it was hot and that I always had to squint my eyes from the sun reflecting off all the glass and new construction.

Dad was so angry, I could see him listening to his own thoughts, the screaming in his head. All his motions were fast and abrupt as though he wanted to smash whatever he touched. I could see the anger in his muscles. He jammed the key in the hotel door, he slammed his bag into a chair. He turned to face me and with open hands and his arms like engine pistons he rammed the butt of both palms into my chest and launched me horizontal back over the bed and my body crumpled in a tangle at the headboard.

I had an upside-down view of him. He stared down at me. I lay in a pile with legs overhead but afraid to move at all. His face was twisted and he wanted to continue to beat me.

I still observed the little things and I noticed he seemed to be running the calculation in his head of how much a beating would set back my training. He had enough calm to run this calculation and it saved me. "I don't like you seeing this girl, Liz. Not until you get a handle on yourself." He walked out of the hotel room and left me there. We had no flight booked because we hadn't anticipated losing so early. Dad came back five hours later with dinner, acting nice and talking about how to get my game back on track. He hugged me, told me he loved me. He told me Liz seemed nice enough but he was worried about me.

I kept losing, the entire season. I'd start a match knowing I was the better player, that I should win, even expecting to win. Anyone watching the match would see my game was far more explosive, that I was strong from both sides on the ground, moved well, volleyed well, huge serve. If they watched a few minutes, they'd guess I'd win in straight sets, easy.

But somewhere early in the match I'd start to slip. I'd make some bad errors, force some dumb shots, get tight. I could feel it drift over me like a fog through the city, choking me. It got so I expected it to come. The way each day the fog rolls toward the Golden Gate then consumes it, I would look for it to come for me. I waited for it. Relented to it. Once it came, I wanted only for the match to end quickly. I'd force more shots, make more errors, accelerate my downfall. I knew I didn't have the mental strength to recover, to reverse the slide.

I came to dread matches, like a person afraid to sleep because he knows a nightmare is waiting.

Dad saw all this happening but didn't know how to stop it and that scared him. He hated to go outside for help. He never intended to do it but he was scared enough that he started a search for a full-time coach for me. Dad was so uncertain of himself at this point that he didn't trust himself to conduct the interviews. He just took the coach most highly recommended for a junior player and paid him exactly what he asked to come work with us in Pennsylvania.

His name was Gabe Sanchez. He wore shorts no matter what the temperature. When he walked his calves would flex into a ball the size of a child's head. His thighs were proportionally large. He was only 5'9" and I don't think any pants were cut in a way to fit his legs.

He was in his late forties then and had been the number one–ranked player in Argentina about twenty-five years earlier, had some Davis Cup wins. He never had big weapons in his game but had a reputation as a tenacious, grind-it-out player who never beat himself, ran down balls, made his opponent hit winners and wore down the other player both physically and mentally.

He was the exact opposite kind of player from me, but I realized this made some sense. What I had couldn't be taught. What I needed, he could teach me.

He loved my serve. He would say that if he had my serve as a twenty-year-old, he would have won the French Open.

I liked Gabe right away. He believed in working hard but also had a Latin love of life. He always smiled and I loved his accent. In all the years I've known Gabe he either started or ended a conversation by saying, "*Arriba, arriba.*" It was something he'd committed to doing as a player and a coach. Just words, a phrase to say, and it became a discipline. Players could create positive energy out of habits and positive energy is a required ingredient for winning. So I would say "*Arriba*" back and I think it helped.

Some parents feel their position of unconditional love permits unfettered abuse. They can rationalize self-forgiveness for harsh treatment because parenting is an obligation and only the parent can do certain things. That's how Dad saw it.

Gabe was the hired coach and I knew he'd be tough and would never abuse. It was a great change for me.

Gabe and I would hit balls for two hours in the morning while Dad watched. Then Gabe and I would have lunch together and talk tennis while Dad left us alone, then we'd hit for two more hours.

After a week of workouts, Mom, Dad, Gabe and I sat for a meeting in the living room while Panos pretended to do homework in the next room.

Gabe said, "We have an unhappy player."

It sounded like a medical condition and I guess it was. Gabe said nothing more while we all looked at each other wondering if this was as serious as cancer. Then Dad said, "What does that mean?"

Gabe leaned forward. "It means we have a decision to make. Anton has a decision. You have a decision. I always insist on having these talks with the entire family with everything out in the open because this decision affects the whole family."

"What's the decision?" said Dad. He always wanted facts, yes-or-no questions. He needed to keep things moving forward. Mom would have asked for all sorts of context and been nonlinear, but not if Dad was around.

"This is a common crossroads for a young teen player," said Gabe. "You need to decide how hard you want to go after it."

"You mean whether he's going to keep playing tennis?" said Dad. I could tell he was wondering if Gabe's approach was a motivational tactic. He couldn't imagine this question as anything other than rhetorical. It was like asking Dad if he planned on taking his next breath.

Gabe picked up on the same thing. "It's a real question. Mostly for Anton but also for all of you. Panos too. Everyone should think through the answer and not take this lightly."

Dad was wondering if he had been wasting his money on Gabe. "Anton's a great player. He could be truly great. Do you agree with that?"

"I do," said Gabe. "He has the potential to be number one in the world."

Dad's face was delighted. He sat back and his look said prosecution rests.

Gabe had seen plenty of asshole tennis parents and he handled Dad beautifully. He turned to me. "Anton, I don't want you to give me a definitive answer until you're ready. Maybe a few days, maybe a few weeks. Whatever the timing is, it is. But I'd like now to hear what you think. Your first reaction."

I didn't have an answer ready. I felt like I was thrown on the podium in front of hundreds of people with no speech ready and no pants on. I realized I'd never seriously been asked the question before. I always knew I hated tennis but I always thought the answer to the question of playing had to be yes.

I said, "I don't know, Gabe." I started and stopped answers and stammered for a while. I wasn't sure that the option of "no" was real. Dad would just fire Gabe and pull me back in, do more research on the next coach he hired.

"Okay," said Gabe. "I understand. Take your time. Just know that if you say yes, it's an absolute yes. I need you all the way in with me and I want you to have fun. Do you understand?"

"I do."

"So I want to propose a third option," said Gabe.

We all stared at Gabe. Panos too. I could tell Dad was thinking what the hell next.

Gabe said, "Give me everything you have, everything. Show up early, work hard, stay late, laugh, enjoy it. Pour your soul into this with me." He paused and stared back at me. "For one year. Everything and for one year. Then you can stop or you can do it for one year more."

It was such a simple thing and I knew it was really a kind of trick anyway but it sounded so good to me. It took me out of the endless, hopeless darkness and gave me a light. It was an escape hatch. I could do anything for one year, and already the time with Gabe was better than the time with Dad.

Dad looked satisfied. Mom was silent and seemed relieved looking at Dad.

"Okay," said Gabe. "One more thing. A hypothetical thing in case the family answer is yes."

"Alright," said Dad.

"I would like you to find a sports psychologist to work with Anton. There should be no stigma attached to psychotherapy. It's an important thing and many successful athletes do this."

We'd never thought about this before so we had no ready answer. Dad wanted to say no right away but knew he would sound like a brute so he said, "I'll think about it."

Gabe said, "I cannot recommend this strongly enough. It is an important step for a dedicated professional athlete. Most do it at some point and it's better to do it early. As in pain anesthesia, it's important to stay ahead of the pain. The best time for therapy is before a crisis."

I never thought anything good or bad about therapy. I was just always up for somebody new to talk with. Dad was old-school so I could tell he didn't like the idea but I could also see that he was starting to believe in Gabe.

The time of day that I would call my own began at 9:30pm, after I'd been fed the right amount of calories, done my stretching exercises and climbed into bed. Sometimes I would read, sometimes I would lie on my back with the sheets up to my ribs, my hands behind my head, and I'd stare up at the ceiling until it became a dark sky filled with stars over my campsite in the wilderness, or a sunset on the horizon of the Caribbean Sea as I'd sit in the sand with my back against the trunk of a palm tree.

For a time, I abandoned the self-flagellating, wallowing-in-loneliness routine and my addiction was the 9:30pm dial of Liz's phone number. She wasn't on a strict get-your-eight-hours-sleep schedule and so wasn't always home and available, but often was and I loved our calls. Connection with a person validated my personhood. Sometimes we spoke only a moment, sometimes much more.

"You have to win this week so I can come watch your match on Saturday."

"Consider it done."

"Good. I'm going to train up to New York to meet a friend and will drive out. Are you coming home in between or staying up there?"

"It's a three-hour drive one way which is too far. I'll be in a hotel starting tomorrow."

"With your dad?"

"Yup."

We each held our phone silently for a moment then she said, "I love watching you play. I always feel proud of you. Attracted to you."

"That's nice to hear." And it was.

"In a way, you're like I was five years ago. With the violin. My mom was the Caucasian, Main Line version of a tiger mom and she got it in her head that I could be a concert violinist and go study at Juilliard."

"I didn't know that."

"It was a long time ago," she said with the youthful gravity and perspective that adults find cute. "I managed to put an end to it, but it had gone on for years. Five hours on Saturdays, five on Sundays, three in the afternoons Monday through Friday. I got pretty good because how could I not, but I wasn't a natural. And I hated, hated, hated it."

"How did you get her to let up on you?"

"You have to prove you aren't gifted. You have to demonstrate to your parents beyond a reasonable doubt that you have no aptitude for excellence in anything at all."

"You tanked your play?"

"It's the teachers too, if you have a good one. A strong one, enough that they can give the parents the truth. They see so many kids, they can see things more clearly than the parents. Every mom and dad thinks their kid has some kind of gift. My teacher told my mom I was pretty good but never headed to Juilliard."

"And your mom backed off."

"That, and I said if she made me keep up with the lessons and practice that she would only make me hate her. Then she backed off. But it was almost five unhappy years of yelling and crying and smashing violins against walls."

I pictured the twelve-year-old version of Liz smashing a violin to the ground like a carnival-goer with a hammer, ringing the bell at the strongman game. "Good for you."

"Parents are so crazy now. Poor parents want their kids to be pro athletes and make lots of money. Rich parents want their kids to do something artsy and exciting and not for the money instead of the tedious lawyer and doctor jobs that they have and they hate. That way they feel that their riches matter for something."

I could have talked to Liz all night. Our phone conversation was the altar of my goddess of salvation. She had fought and bled for her freedom to control her schedule, to sneak to the homes of travelling parents and drink beer on weeknights. "Except my parents are rich and they want me to be a pro athlete."

"Tennis is a country club sport. You're in a crossover category. There are lots more upper class people with extra money for private coaching. Every guy I've ever been friends with has had outside coaching for soccer, lacrosse or tennis. It's a whole cottage industry, these coaches. Probably what my friends will end up doing for work after college. Your situation is more intense than it was for me and for any of them. You're different."

"How so?"

"You actually are gifted."

It was a nice compliment. I liked hearing her use the word in connection with me. I wasn't sure if it was also advice. "So you think I keep going with tennis?"

"Maybe you do. It's hard to be a concert pianist, a NASA scientist or a professional tennis player and also be a functioning social human being. So I don't know. But you do have a gift."

The compliment had gotten cloudy. "Ouch." Liz knew how to sail and to surf, she took road trips with friends, drank beer, smoked pot and cut classes.

"I don't mean autism," she said. "I just mean doing other stuff."

Mom had always said that girls mature faster than boys, that teenage girls can lead teenage boys around on a string. "How is it you know so much?"

"Don't listen to me. I'm just blathering on. And I'm really not even a very good person."

That sounded dangerous and attractive. "Could've fooled me."

"Maybe I have."

Liz's parents were in Bermuda for a long weekend. We'd been dating eight months and she was a high school senior and allowed to look after herself for a few days. I planned to be at her house as much as I could get away.

We would see each other only about once a week but we talked on the phone every night which became part of my calming ritual, like reading a book at bedtime. She liked that she had the power to be therapeutic and she thought of herself as being a part of my team. Sometimes she would sing to me at the end of our call. Our lives had so little in common and that strengthened our bond.

It was October and the fall weather with gentle sun and no humidity had arrived. On Saturday morning I told Dad I was going to drive to Valley Forge Park and jog there. I got in the car and drove directly to Liz's house, my hands vibrating with excitement, uncertainty. We still hadn't had sex other than hand-jobs, and I thought this might be the day.

I parked on the street two doors down because I didn't want the neighbors reporting back to her parents that my car had been in the driveway. Liz and I had agreed on that plan. I walked across her lawn to the front door which was open six inches and I stepped inside.

"Hello?" The living room was dark. I'd been inside the house only once before and didn't know my way around. "Hello?" I said again.

Still nothing. There was a formal dining room to my left and a living room to my right with the staircase directly ahead. On one side of the staircase was a powder room and on the other a coat closet.

"Liz?" I figured the living room was the best place to start so I turned right.

"Boo!" Liz had flung open the closet door and stepped out wearing her dad's navy trench coat that was long enough on her to dust the floor.

I jumped and spun in the air. "Jesus." I had already been on edge.

"A strange man in my house." She took unnatural pleasure in scaring the wits out of me. It didn't have the feel of a prank to be mutually enjoyed. It felt more like the thoughtless amusement of burning ants with a magnifying glass.

I smiled. "You shouldn't leave your door open."

The next act in her script was more enjoyable. "What are you going to do to me?" She unbuttoned the trench coat and arched her shoulders to let it slide down to her feet. She was wearing a black one-piece thong teddy. She did a three-sixty then walked backwards to me, pressing her ass into me and bent forward to put her hands to her knees.

"I could think of a few things."

"Bad boy. Breaking and entering. Taking advantage of a girl home alone."

"Right."

She straightened, turned and put her hands on my chest. "Then let's get this over with."

She dropped to her knees in front of me and yanked my jogging shorts to my feet. She took me in her mouth and began the slow rocking back and forth of her jaw over me, urging on my erection. I was still preoccupied with the earlier peek-a-boo and hadn't caught up with the transition. Her efforts felt undeniably phenomenal but to no visible effect. It was as though someone had cut the nerve, dammed up the river, closed the valve.

I concentrated, tried to translate those wonderful sensations to an erect state of readiness as a show of my appreciation, but the more I concentrated, the more pressure I felt and the more hopeless things became.

She began to make soft grunts of confusion and frustration. Her annoyance grew to the point of a pause and full harrumph, but she didn't give up. She came back on me with game perseverance until finally I felt a tingle. A promising accumulation of blood flow.

I could sense that she sensed it as well and she began to work more furiously, determined to be victorious and keep what must have been a perfect record of male arousal.

Her momentum built, as did mine, and in a moment I was fully erect.

She leaned back and held me up like a jeweler showing a pocket watch on a chain and instructed, "It should come to me in this condition."

From there it took her less than two minutes to finish me off.

She stood and looked up into my eyes. "What a wonderful intruder you are."

"Wow, Liz."

She laughed. "Better than jogging in Valley Forge Park?"

"Well, it's different. And a million times better."

"You want a beer?"

"No, I better not." Don't be an ass. This was a moment. First blow job. "Actually I'll have one. Sounds good."

She went to the kitchen, still wearing the black thong, and came back with two Bud bottles. I wondered what sex would feel like.

"So we're on for tonight?" she said.

"Yup."

"What's the plan?"

"Still a surprise, you'll see soon enough." I had tickets to see the Dave Matthews Band at the Mann Music Center, an outdoor amphitheater.

"Sorry we can't get started sooner, but, you know, we cheerleaders have responsibilities."

"I know. I wouldn't want the football team to have no cheers."

"It's alumni weekend. Bunch of old people walking around. Meet you here after? Around seven?"

"Great."

I was sitting next to her on the sofa of the living room. She pivoted over me to straddle my lap and wrapped her arms around my head. She gave me a long kiss with relaxed lips and an active tongue.

"Anton, you are such a good person and I love you. I always thought it would be ignorant and provincial to marry a high school sweetheart, but here I am, in love with you. What else can you do when you meet your soul mate in high school? You're the love of my life."

I pulled her in for more kissing. I held her hips and moved her back and forth over me in a rhythm that was the closest I'd been to sex. I was hard again. Good to be sixteen.

"I have to get ready, Lover," she said. "I'll see you at seven."

After the beer I jogged anyway then hit some balls with Dad and by four o'clock was showered, dressed and bored so I decided to check out my beautiful girlfriend in her cheerleader outfit. Dad was on the sofa watching a Phillies game while Mom read a book in her bedroom.

I got to the game in the fourth quarter and a sea of people circled the football field. I stood rows back near the corner of one end zone and could see Liz but barely. She wore a vest and a miniskirt and pom poms in the red and white school colors. The home team was up 28–14 and everyone was happy on our side.

At the final whistle the players ran to midfield and the cheerleaders turned to the crowd behind the home sideline and waved pom poms. The crowd stayed thick, talking about the good win for the program. I worked my way toward the field but in a moment the players went off in a jog to the gym followed by jogging cheerleaders.

I knew the layout of the school but none of the people so I kept making slow progress to where I knew the gym and the locker rooms to be. Kids streamed in and out of the buildings so I walked as though I could be one of them.

Near the women's locker room a girl's voice said, "Anton!"

I turned to see a cheerleader. She was still in her cheerleader outfit and had put a trench coat over it. I recognized her from the eighth grade years ago, but couldn't remember her name. "Hi."

"Good to see you. How are you?"

"Good, things are good. Still in the area."

"Great. Gosh, I haven't seen you in so long. What are you doing here?"

"I'm looking for Liz."

"Liz Betterton?"

"Yeah."

"Oh." She looked curious, or maybe disappointed. "Okay. Well, she's not in here," and she thumbed toward the women's locker room behind her. "She was walking to the pool last I saw her." She adjusted the shoulders of her coat and hustled off.

"Thanks." Erica, I remembered her name, too late.

I walked down the corridor toward the pool, the smell of chlorine getting stronger as I went. The way was bright with fluorescent lighting but no one was around. The men's and women's locker rooms were in the opposite direction.

At the end of the corridor, two metal swinging doors led to the pool. I pushed through to warmer air heavy with pool chemicals. Fifteen feet ahead were two cheerleaders by the pool's edge, talking and smoking cigarettes.

"Hi," I said and walked up to them.

They froze and went silent, the only animation the trail of smoke from the tips of the cigarettes now dangling from inattentive fingers.

I stopped right in front of them, forming a tight triangle. "Have you seen Liz Betterton?"

They kept staring at me. I didn't recognize them but wondered if they recognized me. Finally one said, "OMG."

The other said, "Later!" in an unnecessarily loud voice and they forced their way toward the swinging doors behind me. I thought I heard laughter from the corridor. The cheerleaders had been standing in front of a door to the room for all the swim team equipment and training tables. I heard muted voices from inside. Fearing what was on the other side but not giving any conscious thought to what the source of fear might be, I turned the knob and pushed the door open wide.

Two heads turned to me in alarmed synchronization. One was Liz Betterton, still in her cheerleader uniform, but with her skirt raised over her lower back while she bent forward and rested her elbows on the training table. Behind and inside her was a football player, also still in uniform. Number eleven. No helmet but eye black, shoulder pads and jersey, his football pants in a puddle around his cleated feet.

Liz's face went from surprise to fear and I knew at once that it was fear for herself and reputation, not fear for damage to me. The football player's face went from surprise to amusement. He said, "Hey, buddy, what the hell? Beat it." He showed no recognition of who I was or even that there could be another competing for Liz.

Number eleven. It occurred to me in that moment that this was the punter, a fact I confirmed in the obsessive and depressive months that followed, using a team program. The damn punter.

I stepped back, leaving the pool, the gym and the school, the equipment room door still open so they'd have to untangle first if they wanted privacy again.

I walked to my car which was parked on a street off campus and realized then that I had never been the boyfriend. Not the primary. I had never parked in her driveway but down the street. I didn't speak with her parents because they thought she was dating someone else. She wasn't interested in meeting mine. Our routine wasn't a rebellion. It was a fraud.

I had been unpracticed in the art of socialization. I didn't know enough honest people and dishonest people so I had never learned to tell the difference. I knew one girl and she turned out to be dishonest. Brutally so.

I drove from campus knowing I'd never return. My window away from tennis that had been full of light was bricked over. So I returned to tennis the way a bulimic returns to the bathroom having been called fat. Dad won another round.

The woman I thought of as a kind of salvation, who had gotten a closer look at me than anyone else, found me interesting only as a toy on the side while she dated the punter. I was an oddity, a dropout, an Elephant Man.

Mom and Dad knew Liz only from what they saw through the living room window as we would drive off. They didn't ask after her much and so I spent two days numb and feeling more alone, surrounded by people I couldn't reach and who couldn't reach me. On the third morning Mom stood alone in the kitchen when I walked in. Dad was out for a breakfast meeting with an investment advisor. There was a big difference between Dad being out of the room and out of the house altogether. A feeling of the military at-ease command when you knew he wouldn't drop in at any moment.

Mom was still so beautiful. She could have been a soap opera star. I didn't want to talk about Liz. Didn't know how to. "Do you think I should play tennis?" I said. I still hadn't given Gabe the official answer.

"Oh, that's your decision, honey."

"I know that." I didn't know that at all. "But what do you think?"

"I think you have tremendous gifts. You can be a beautiful player. You are already, and it can open up a world of experiences to you."

I nodded.

"I got to have an Olympic experience, travel to incredible places, compete, meet new people, all at a young age. I'd like for you to have experiences like that."

"What do I have to give up?"

She made a sweet, sad smile. I'd say it was in response to my question but she always seemed to have a sweet, sad smile. She did take a very long time to answer, though. "A casual life."

I knew what she meant. "Yeah," I said.

"One year with Gabe sounds very reasonable."

I nodded.

"Anton, if you stop fighting your father, if you support him, most of the difficulties will go away. It will be so much easier if you go along with it."

"If I surrender to it."

"No, that's not what I mean." Her voice didn't get louder but it got harder. I didn't know how much she loved Dad. It wasn't the kind of love affair teen girls dream about but I guessed she loved him and was loyal to him and wouldn't criticize him. "I mean work alongside him. Work together."

"Together," I repeated to my shoes.

"Anton, he wants what's best for you. There's nothing wrong with that. Don't you want that also?"

"Who gets to determine what's best for me?"

I think she had wanted not to tell me what to do, to let it be all my decision, but she was struggling with that and I had given her an out. "You asked my opinion. I think a year of dedicating yourself to tennis is what you should do."

We heard steps in the hallway. Panos was slapping his shoes on the hardwood extra loud as a courtesy to let us know he was coming. We waited the few seconds in silence to let him come.

Panos and Mom were closer than me and Mom. They got to spend a lot of time together since Dad was always with me pushing tennis. Panos was great at breaking tension and he knew how to make Mom happy. He pressed his hands over her ears and pulled her forehead in for a kiss, then he smacked her bottom on the way to the refrigerator.

"What's doin', mama-san?" he said.

I laughed. He had a great older-brother style.

"Your brother and I are talking about Gabe's proposal."

"Yes, the decent proposal." He drank milk from the carton directly.

I hated when he did that. No one else in the family did that. "Christ, Panos. Get a glass. Disgusting."

He had more from the carton and made sure some dripped down his chin. "Pretty boy," he said to me.

Mom took the opportunity. "Why don't you boys talk for a while." She left the room.

Panos waited until we couldn't hear her steps. "What did she tell you?"

"Take the deal." If I really wanted to talk about Liz, Panos was the only choice, but I didn't want to put into words the details of what I had seen. The humiliation and the actual hurt were worse than silent suffering. She was just another thing I couldn't talk about with anyone.

"Yeah." He put the milk away. "She has to. You know that, right?"

I wasn't ready to concede that. "Aren't you ever pissed at Mom? Disappointed?" Better just to talk about tennis, Mom and Dad. What used to cause choking claustrophobia now felt like a safe place compared to the acute crisis of Liz.

Panos sat at the breakfast table across from me. He had no idea that anything else was consuming my thoughts. He couldn't have. Tennis was plenty to explain any upset I showed. He loved Mom and he loved me. He reached over the table and put his hand on my upper arm. "Mom tries. She does things, things behind the scenes, more than you know. It's not easy. It puts some of the heat on her but it takes some off you. Nobody can change Dad. All anyone can do is try to soften things a little."

I nodded.

"I'll tell you a little secret."

"Okay."

"You'll find out soon enough anyway. She enrolled in classes to get a degree in child psychology."

"That's good. That'll give her some independence, something outside the house," I said.

"It's a way for her to take some power back. With you."

I knew what he meant. It wasn't power back from me. It was power back from Dad regarding me. "You think it's about my childhood or her own?" I was still struggling to parallel-process my flash fire with Liz and the slow burn of tennis.

"Both. You're definitely a lot of it. She loves you, she cares. She's trying to figure out a way. She used to be more of a match for Dad but when one person in a relationship takes charge more often that becomes a pattern, then the pattern creates roles for the people in the relationship and over years people move deeper into their roles. It's not that she's been beaten down, really. But she allowed this to be her role." Panos shrugged. "Beneath all that, she's in your corner. She wants what's best for you. Right now she thinks that's tennis."

"I guess so." I looked at Panos then out the kitchen window. "So of course I'm going to take the deal."

"Of course," he said. "And it was never a deal anyway. Maybe Gabe thought so, but I bet he's too smart for that. It was always an ultimatum. A softened ultimatum."

"One year."

"Right."

"Do you think I can stop after one year if I want?"

"You'd have to put up a major stink."

"I might." Although the one-year bargain was less important to me than it was before the Saturday football game. I might want to bury my head even longer than that.

"You might." He nodded. "Anton, taking it one year at a time is a good approach. It's a good way to think about it." He was deciding whether or not to tell me his next thought. He decided yes. "There's something you should also get used to. I used to think you'd have to play until you lost. Until your ranking got so low and hopeless, but that won't be the end. Dad knows what a great player you are, he's seen it. We all have. You'll play until you play your best, then your best will win and you can't stop until your best can't win anymore. You're going to be playing tennis for a long time."

"Unless I go nuclear."

Panos nodded. "You could. And you'd still have a brother in your life. But that's all."

I filled my lungs and exhaled all of it through my teeth. "One year at a time," I said.

"Can you do it?"

"I just might be able to trick myself into doing it."

Two hours later Dad got home. He announced he had hired a sports psychologist and I had an appointment the next morning.

CHAPTER

11

The next morning I woke to my mother sitting on the side of my bed, staring into my blinking eyes as I focused and tried to distinguish dream from day. "Mom?"

Her hand was resting on my chest over my heart. "Good morning."

I pushed myself up so that I was leaning back on my elbows. "What's up?"

"I wanted to apologize to you for what I said yesterday. I didn't handle that well. I shouldn't have told you what to do."

"I asked you what you thought. It's fine, Mom. Don't worry about it."

"The truth is I don't know what you should do. Which is more reason that I shouldn't have answered." She cleared her throat and started in on what she wanted to tell me and I could tell she had rehearsed the first line of it. "The clearest memories I have from when I was less than ten years old have nothing to do with birthday parties or vacations or barreling down a ski slope. The clearest memories I have are the times I would go to my mother on a rainy day in Minnesota and complain that I was bored. Do you know what she'd say? She'd say 'Good.' "

"That's not very helpful."

"It was, though. She'd say, 'Good, I'm looking forward to see-ing what you do about that.' "

"What's so memorable about that?"

"It's memorable because even then I recognized what a gift that was. The gift to learn how to do it myself. To grow, imagine. It's a gift I've never been able to give to you."

It felt as though she was unloading her regrets on me which was doubly unfair. "I'm doing fine, Mom."

"Are you? How can a person be aware of his absence of imagi-nation?"

"It's unimaginable."

She was too busy lamenting her parenting to laugh. "There's great value in spare time, in boredom. Early in life, it's instructive. If it only ever comes late in life, it will be hard because you won't have the tools for it."

She was giving her work and me, her work product, a failing grade. It was a judgment, resigned and sad. I wanted to scream, "And so what now, Mom!," but I knew she had no solution. This was not to be a constructive moment. It was only self-loathing, which I disliked witnessing, and pity for me, which I disliked even more. "Thanks, Mom. Very uplifting."

The whole way to the psychiatrist's office I wondered if there would be a sofa. Instead, there was a wide and very deep stuffed leather

TROPHY SON | 63

chair with fat armrests and I sat all the way back so my legs couldn't bend to ninety degrees. Sitting that way naturally made me feel like a kid in a grown-up chair. I wondered if it was a deliberate tool to get patients in the frame of mind for regressing to childhood memories.

Dad had dropped me in the parking lot in Bryn Mawr and driven off to get coffee, just one town over and about ten minutes from our house. I was buzzed into a small, shared sitting area that fed into a maze of hallways and doctors' offices. Every six feet or so in the halls was a round, white noise dampener about the size of a smoke alarm, except these were on the floor and made the constant static noise of an old-time TV that's turned to no channel at all.

Dr. Ford sat facing me in an office chair on casters and his back to a small desk with only a phone and a pad of paper on it. The room was eight feet by eight feet with one window, no personal photos anywhere and almost nothing on the walls, just a large photo of the ocean. The sea, horizon and sky, not the waves breaking on a beach.

"How are you, Anton?"

"Good."

"In our first session I'll take a lot of notes if that's okay?"

"Of course."

"After that we'll mostly talk and I won't take notes but today we may cover a lot of information."

"Sure."

We covered all my significant relationships, who the characters in my life were. Grandparents, all deceased, parents, Panos, coach, tutor, a couple boys from school I was friends with but hadn't spoken with on the phone in more than a year, a girl from school I thought was good looking but spoke to only a few times and never asked out and hadn't spoken to in more than two years. I mentioned Ben Archer as a tennis rival though I didn't know why I included him as a name for Dr. Ford. I'd never spoken to Ben off a tennis court. I mentioned Liz as an ex-girlfriend and moved right on.

It didn't take long and I wondered if Dr. Ford found the list as short and disturbing as I did but he had a good poker face and I couldn't tell.

He had me start with some of my earliest memories at home, at school, when I first felt love for tennis, first felt hate. I'm so bad at remembering stuff like that, especially on the spot, but I picked some examples. My first school memory was running out of the kindergarten schoolhouse to Mom, who picked me up, and we drove to a field where she had rented a garden plot to grow vege-tables. My first memory at home was helping Mom do a load of laundry and spilling the cup of liquid detergent across the top of the washing machine and we made a game of Zamboni to push the soap into the machine on top of the clothes. The first I felt love for tennis was acing Dad for the first time a few years ago. For hate, I joked I'd have to narrow it down and get back to him. He laughed and let it go at that.

"Do you want to win at tennis?"

I had just downloaded *Bull Durham* and I paraphrased Tim Robbins. "Winning's better than losing."

He smiled. "I think I can help you win. Like many sports, and especially tennis, winning is a mental exercise. If we're honest with each other in here, if the real you shows up each time you're here, I can give you tools to help you win."

"Okay, great," I said. I didn't realize it at the time but this doctor was wrong for me. What he had asked was wrong and I would realize it soon, but I didn't know it then. Asking if I wanted to win at tennis should have been the second question, only if I had already answered yes to the question of whether I wanted to play tennis.

Dr. Ford skipped that part because he worked for Dad, not for me. He made no distinction between the goals of making me a great person and a great tennis player, but that lack of distinction was my whole problem in the first place. Anyway, I didn't understand this yet, and it also felt good just to have a safe place to talk. I talked so little about anything during the usual days. Maybe I could release some of the Liz toxins here. It still made my stomach cramp to conjure the memory.

"How do you feel about your new coach?"

"I like Gabe a lot."

"Do you think you can win with Gabe?"

"I do."

"Why is that? What's different?"

"He really knows the game. Dad knows a lot but he was never a pro, never had formal training. Gabe has already taught me some small things. Subtle things that help. He makes practice a little more fun."

"Good. And is your dad still involved?"

"Sort of. Gabe and I practice at the house so Dad's always there. He's aware of everything but he stays out of it while Gabe's there and sometimes we'll talk after Gabe leaves. He seems to want to give Gabe some room. Dad was an athlete so he respects the player-coach relationship."

"Good. That's good. So would you say you feel supported?"

I hadn't thought about it that way before but I considered that I had a tennis court in our backyard, an expensive coach, plenty of rackets and balls, transportation to any tournament, a dad who was newly giving me some space. "Yes, I think so," I said.

"Will you practice today?"

"At two o'clock."

"What will you be thinking when you step on the court today?"

Gabe had played against Federer, Nadal, Murray when he was younger. He got his ass kicked by all of them but he'd seen them up close. "I want to impress Gabe."

"You want to be a great player," said Dr. Ford.

"I do."

"It'll be a long road. Lots of work," he said. "I think you can do it."

When I saw Gabe at two o'clock that afternoon I told him I was all-in for a year. We shook hands. I stepped on the court with him and played great.

I was winning again. Cruising. Having made the decision to commit helped me focus. I was seeing the ball so well, hitting it so cleanly, putting it anywhere I wanted. I could design a point in my head then make it happen exactly that way, like a playwright. On the court my will became reality and I could see my opponents knew it. They could feel they were just a piece on my game board. I didn't lose even a set the entire summer. Only Ben Archer pushed me to a tie break once which I won, then I won the second set 6–0.

Life off the court was robotic, single-threaded. I was worshipping at Dad's altar. I kept that from bothering me by remembering that I had made a deal with myself and I was getting the results I had bargained for in the deal so everything seemed fine. My time with Liz was now in a sealed vault buried fifty feet underground like an ancient city now forgotten beneath a present-day tennis center.

Dad's whole being was dominated by the one-to-one correlation between his happiness and my winning so he was very happy.

Gabe also was feeling great. In a matter of only weeks he had unlocked my potential and got me winning again.

Mom was happy because there was peace in the house. We had lots of hugs. Hugs and knowing looks like people living carefully under a mad king. Not Anne-Frank-living-in-the-attic type stuff. Just people who don't believe in fascism.

I started reading more, at least two hours every night. I discovered Milan Kundera and Philip Roth. Roth had written a lot of books and for a period of three months I considered him my best friend. I wanted to meet him. I related to him and I wanted to meet him more than I wanted to meet my tennis hero, John McEnroe. McEnroe was an adult, independent with plenty of money, and he still surrounded himself with tennis. I couldn't relate to that at all.

I told this to Dr. Ford. I said it exactly that way. "I think Philip Roth is my best friend."

"Who is Philip Roth?"

"The writer."

"Oh, of course. *The Ghost Writer; My Life as a Man.*"

"Right," I said.

"When did you meet Philip Roth?"

"I haven't."

Dr. Ford never showed confusion. He just took longer to say something, a trait I thought was pretty good and wanted to test. "I see. But you love his writing?"

"Very much."

"And you relate to him in some way?"

"I do," I said.

"More than people?"

"What people?" I said.

"The people in your life."

"I repeat," I said.

Dr. Ford smiled. "Well, that's not entirely fair, Anton."

If I knew then what I know now I'd have told him to shut the fuck up right there. But instead I said, "There are props in my life, not people. Except Panos but he's at college now with a girlfriend and I'm playing all the time. I hardly see him anymore."

"Aren't things with your mother improved? With your father?"

"Everyone has self-awareness of the plan we're on and the plan is like a balm for a cold sore. So, yes, the plan is working as much as a balm can work for a cold sore." I learned more from my novelist friends than from Dr. Ford.

"So, that's very good."

"It's one dimensional. I'm one dimensional."

Ford watched me.

"If I win a match, a tournament, I don't have anyone to share it with. Not really. Gabe and I will high-five and talk about tactical points. Same with Dad. Mom will say congratulations and Panos is away. The best I can do is go up to my room and talk about it with the dust jacket of a Philip Roth novel."

Ford smiled and looked at me. The piece of shit didn't know where to go with this. I suppose it was possible he wanted to talk with me about developing a fuller self and some friendships but knew that's not what Dad wanted. Or maybe he really believed his approach. In any event, it clicked for me that he wasn't helping me, he was helping me play more tennis. He was just as invested in my winning as Gabe and Dad.

He never once engaged me, challenged me in a way that would lead to discovery. All he ever tried to do was calm me down.

I began to resent Dr. Ford. He was another connection to nothing and our meetings became just an obligation for me. Maybe it was doomed with Ford from the start. I had always been suspicious of his being just an emissary from Dad so I was cautious, and you get out of these things only what you put in. I held on to my consciousness of the deal I had willingly struck and on to my books.

13

M y second serve hit an inch inside the corner of the service box. It was loaded with spin and it kicked wide so by the time it was as deep as the baseline it was twelve feet off the court. My opponent in the semis had turned his shoulders to scramble wide but never got close and bowed his head.

Then he straightened up and walked toward the deuce court. I saw him remove despair from his face and replace it with something else. "Long," he said.

I froze. I stared at him but he wouldn't look at me. He kept walking to the deuce court to get ready to return serve again.

"Bullshit," I said under my breath. I saw the ball clearly in and I knew he did too because I saw just as clearly the moment he made up his mind to cheat. There were no linespeople in the semis of a juniors tournament. It was the honor system.

It was a clay court tournament at a country club in Westchester, New York. The courts were right alongside the Long Island

Sound. Boats of many shapes and sizes clung to moorings and dutifully pointed into the wind, geese climbed from the marshy beaches up to the outskirts of the club lawns and honked like damaged trumpets until a man chased them away by opening and closing an umbrella. Club members on their way out for a sail would pause by the courts to watch then fly off like the hundreds of seagulls around us.

He stood behind the baseline twirling his racket until enough time passed that he had to look at me. "Deuce," he said.

"Let me see the mark," I said.

"It was two inches out, at least," he said.

"Let's see it."

I walked around the net and he walked back over to the service box of the ad court. The court was swept before the match and this was only the third game so there were very few ball marks. None was two inches outside the corner.

I saw he was looking hard as he approached. I'm long and work to shorten my steps for my tennis footwork, but he naturally moved in quick, short steps like a small dog. Good for tennis movement. "Where's the mark?" I said.

"There wouldn't be one," he said. "It hit the sideline tape but it hit two inches long."

If a ball hits the tape, the ball is wide enough that usually there is still a small edge mark in the clay around the tape. A ball off the tape also takes a different bounce. Neither of these happened. There was a ball mark right inside the corner of the service box. I circled it using the frame of my racket. "That's my mark."

"Sorry, it's not. It hit the tape back here." He was owning the lie and feeling more confident about it. He knew he'd already gotten away with it.

I stared at him and he shrugged his shoulders. I wanted to grab the hair on the back of his head and scrape his face across the court. He was trying to take something important from me.

He shrugged again to say this wasn't his problem and walked away to return serve. I walked back to the baseline on my side of the court and I murdered the ball, as hard as I'd ever hit a serve, four times in a row, all four out. Game to the cheater. The first service game I'd lost the entire tournament.

I sat at the changeover. I took a towel in my hands and started to lean my face into it, then stopped because I didn't want to show how rattled I was. I sat frozen with the towel across my lap and my hands over it, eyes straight ahead while I tried different conversations with myself to get calm again. It went something like this:

"He fucking cheated me."

"Get it together. It's one game."

"He fucking cheated and he'll cheat again."

"You're twice the player. Play conservative. Beat him."

"You're telling me I need to change my game because he's shrinking the court in half. This is bullshit."

"These are the moments that test us. You're too good to play this guy straight up. This makes it interesting. Get focused and kick his ass."

"Fuck him."

"That's right. Fuck him. Do it on the court."

Tennis players do a lot of inner monologuing and sometimes it creeps out like Tourette's. In our little bubble, we have to be player, coach, confidant, trainer. When all the voices started, it was a reminder of how alone I was.

I lost the next three games before I could talk myself into focus. I evened the set at six games each and got into a tiebreaker.

He served first into the deuce court and I ripped a forehand up the line that he never had a chance at reaching. I was up a mini-break.

I missed my first serve into the ad court but pegged an aggressive second serve that he couldn't get a racket on. I was up 2-0 in the breaker except I heard, "Out." It was the same ad court as his last cheat.

I had been in a rage earlier in the set and I was right back there, faster this time having travelled there before. "That serve was in you piece of shit."

"It was out." He smiled. "Two inches."

I refused to look to Dad for help but I needed help. I was losing it. I needed to check my language. Another curse could get an official over here to disqualify me. I was lucky not to lose points for the one I already let fly.

I dropped my racket in defiance and my fists were balled up. I never fought but right then it seemed like it would be so easy and feel so good. I imagined smashing my fist in his face over and over. I stood staring and kept imagining it.

He walked to the deuce court, twirling his racket and having fun. He took his time, enjoying the manipulation. I was powerless again. Nowhere for my fury to release. I walked back to the baseline and I told myself not to over-hit.

I took my time settling in for the serve. I bounced the ball in front of me, took deep breaths, envisioned laying in a nice, easy serve. Nothing mattered, though. I double-faulted away the point and collapsed in the tiebreak, 7–1.

The second set I lost in a blur. He cheated one more time but didn't need to. I was mentally done and wanted off the court. My match win streak ended and I would have played Ben Archer in the final. Ben won the tournament. I didn't stick around to see if the other guy cheated any.

It was the first I thought of Ben as possibly more than just a less talented me. I had more talent and was certain of that, but he had an entirely different approach, a more steady approach. I wasn't the faster of two hares. He was a tortoise and might win a long race.

I had walked off the court from the match and Dad stood there waiting for me. It was the first and last time he wasn't angry with me after a loss. His eyes were savage while he watched the other player and coach. There was just enough civilization present around us to hold Dad back, otherwise I think he would have killed that boy.

Two days later I slouched deep in the chair in Dr. Ford's office. I didn't see him on any kind of regular basis because I'd been pretending that it was working and that I was feeling much healthier. Even so, we tried not to let more than a month go by between visits.

I was still upset from the match I had lost and so my guard was down. I didn't check my honesty and openness but let everything come forward. I took him through the match, almost point by point. I relayed the conversations that happened when the other player cheated and how I had struggled to conquer my anger and fear of losing. I told him how winning never feels as good as losing feels bad and when he asked why, I told him that my wins were for someone else but my losses were all on me.

He told me I had passion and valued winning and that's the mark of a champion.

I thought about that for a while in silence. No champion has ever won every time out. Everyone has felt the sting of knowing that he could have won one more. That's competition, I understand that. But unhappy? Lasting and deep down where it counts? I thought that might be something else.

I said, "The thing I want to change is that when I lose a match, I don't only lose confidence in myself as a player, I lose confidence in myself as a person."

He nodded to me and said, "Your losses have to build your character. You have to learn from them, take that and build on it."

Stock answer. I could have gotten that from embroidery on a pillow. "Doctor, what I'm saying is that my self as a player is my whole self. When I lose, there's no other part of me to fall back on. There's no other self to retreat to. I'm trapped. It's claustrophobic." I pictured the spirit of me caught in the small confines of my skull, pushing like a child on the walls of a burning house, gasping for air.

Dr. Ford looked frustrated. What kind of prick shrink would get frustrated with a patient who said what I just finished saying? "Winning is why you work hard. Let's give you some tools to get you back to work."

Dr. Ford would never change the framework. He would never move the value from winning at tennis to happiness in life. He seemed to feel that if he never acknowledged my unhappiness but pointed elsewhere that the unhappiness would be gone. A matter of a simple Jedi Mind Trick, as long as I won tournaments.

I decided that I'd attend meetings with Dr. Ford but would never work at them. Dr. Ford was a bad investment of my time. Worse, I knew he wasn't on my side.

It would be better to work at this alone. There was thinking that I didn't share with Dr. Ford. Observing, really. In my match with that jerk, I didn't cheat in response. I was happy about that. I didn't know why I didn't cheat. It wasn't a decision that I made. It never occurred to me as an option. Years later I would look back on it and think, how obvious, how stupid not to fight fire with fire, you fuck with me and I fuck with you. But my behavior then was innocent and that's reassuring to me, because of course later the cheating would come, fighting fire with fire. But that wasn't about line calls.

14

It was time to start acting like the player everyone expected that I would be in twelve months. Dad said I needed to start acting like a pro, feeling like a pro, then I'd start playing like a pro. Gabe agreed. He thought putting on all the trappings of a star now would prepare me for becoming a star. And Dad could afford it.

Gabe used to string all my rackets but we hired a racket stringer. It was absurd. I needed maybe twelve rackets strung each week which Gabe or I could easily do, but for big tournaments our stringer would travel with us and be a part of my entourage, mostly for the sake of having an entourage at all.

His name was Adam Hennes and he loved surfing more than tennis. He'd been a decent college player, then a teaching pro at a private tennis club but was fired, as I found out later, because he loved the female membership even more than surfing. He was taking some time off and he knew Gabe somehow and agreed to make some extra money stringing for me.

The first day he came by our house in jeans and a concert T-shirt which is about what he always wore unless we travelled. He had long blond hair and looked like the front man of a grunge band.

I liked him a lot and came to realize that Gabe knew I would. Adam was easy company. He was amused by life and any version of it, so he had no agenda other than to take what came. He was stoned most of the time. I wasn't so naïve as not to recognize that, and of course Gabe knew also. This was never discussed and the rule Gabe gave Adam was that he was never permitted to light a joint around me. Gabe would tolerate Adam with a buzz as long as the smoking was out of sight.

Adam knew enough about competitive tennis to relate to me. I didn't view him as having failed out of tennis. I viewed him as a survivor, even a success story. He was happy.

The other hire to our entourage was our trainer, Bobby Hicks. He was about fifty. Too old for the amount of tan and muscle he had, and certainly too old for the ponytail, but he was a well-known and expensive trainer. He'd worked mostly with major league baseball players and Dad paid him as much as a Yankee would.

Now I had infrastructure, a team around me. Gabe, Bobby, Adam and Dad. They were supposed to help me get ready for the tennis court but I thought they might also be able to help me in other ways. At least there were more people to talk to.

We'd travel to small towns to play Challenger events. Sunrise, Plantation, Calabasas, Rochester, Tulsa, Wichita, Godfrey, Decatur, Champaign, Birmingham, Pensacola. There'd be young up-and-comers like me or slightly older up-and-comers, and some much older guys on the way down trying to hang on to the game. Some of the older guys had held a top-100 world ranking in years past, before age, injury and burnout. Even those guys didn't have the money for a team around them.

We pulled into the Marriott in Reston, Virginia, in the black Suburban that Dad rented. It was a large circular drive with a carport over the lobby entrance and hardscaping all around the front with landscaped flowering trees that couldn't be indigenous. The five of us climbed out and unloaded luggage and bags of tennis equipment while players, guests and hotel employees watched the car waiting for a celebrity to get out next. When they realized the car was empty, they scanned the five of us to see who they should recognize. With my infrastructure all checking in to see that I was okay, onlookers realized that this was my team. Making me someone to watch in the parking lot made me someone to watch on the court. I had to get used to it sooner or later. So went the thinking.

"Big Gabe, what's the schedule?" said Adam.

"Anton, we have a practice court in thirty minutes. We'll do a ninety-minute light workout, then you have a sixty-minute warm down and stretching with Bobby."

I nodded.

Adam said, "Thirty and ninety and sixty. Anton-Atom-Bomb, I will have the PlayStation up and running in the suite in one-eighty."

Something to look forward to. "I'll be there," I said.

Adam left to get stoned and find something to eat. He'd have several new friends by the time I next saw him. Could be a travelling business executive, a player's parent or a homeless person. Adam didn't judge others. He just liked people, all shapes, sizes, types. That's also why he didn't really judge himself, which has to be an easier way to go through life, if you're okay with it. Adam was the person most receptive to help I'd ever seen. The help could be advice, narcotics, a free lunch. He was very accepting.

That day I practiced, stretched and got a massage, then played Adam in PlayStation back at the hotel. I walked to the suite window and looked down at the brownish-orange roof of the carport and the landscaping around the drive. Sprinklers rose from the mulching like submarine periscopes and began painting the shrubs with water. The next day was the same except instead of practicing ninety minutes, I won a match in less than sixty. Back in the hotel I walked to the suite window at exactly the same time and was able to confirm that the sprinklers were on a timer. Every day that week was the same until I won the tournament and we left.

Then we played more tournaments and I won those too. People were starting to know who I was even without the entourage.

More winning meant not only more tournaments on my schedule, but also more matches at every tournament. Instead of an early round loss, then a few days off, I won and played matches through the end of the week then flew off to play another.

There are impact workouts and non-impact workouts. Impact happens when you jam your feet to the hard court in order to stop and change direction. That kind of impact breaks down the body. Non-impact is riding a stationary bike. I could work myself to the bone with non-impact and still recover because I was a teenager. But even then, the impact was getting tough. I was taking on the rigor of a pro schedule and I could feel my body starting to break down, starving for recovery time.

It occurred to me in several tournaments that I could tank an early round match to get some rest but I knew my body would give out before my mind would. I was learning that one of the tests of a pro schedule was endurance over the long haul. The beating of an eleven-month tennis season. I would need a better plan.

L ie down on the table," said Bobby. "I'll get the ice."
"It feels like someone jabbed a pitchfork through my lower back."

"Just relax. Don't move."

"I don't think I can move." I was back in Florida where I played so many of my tournaments at that time. The muscles in my lower back had been quivering like the plucked string of a bow the entire third set with occasional seizures of sharp pain. I moved carefully, gingerly during the match. Swung my racket without aggression. It wasn't enough and I lost in the second round. I had lost in the third round of the tournament before. Both my back and my shoulder had been giving me problems.

"I'm going to massage it out gently for a few minutes, then we'll go to the ice."

Bobby pressed his thumbs into the muscles along the sides of my spinal column and my back signaled maximum pain to my brain. "Too hard, too hard," I yelled.

"Okay." He pulled back his thumbs. My muscles were raw and angry. Bobby used the heel of his palms to rub up and down over my lower back which still hurt like hell. Then he draped a large plastic bag of ice directly over the skin of my back and I could feel the ice drinking in the intense heat from me.

The relief came fast but the idea of serving a tennis ball was outrageous, like the eighty-year-old man on a park bench watching the kids at play and wishing for just one more day of pain-free movement. Except I was a month before my eighteenth birthday. "My body's breaking down, Bobby."

"Yup," he said.

"Ever since we stepped up my schedule, I can't take it. I can't recover enough to play well."

"We'll work it out," he said.

I had started to think I didn't have a pro body. They talked about it in the NBA all the time. So-and-so is built strong, has an NBA body, can take the pounding. "It's not like I can train my way out of it. That's just more abuse I'd have to recover from."

"We'll come up with a plan."

"Should I take time off the tour? Train and try to get stronger, then come back? Maybe I'm too young for the schedule."

"You're not too young."

"Well I'm not doing it. I'm not succeeding. This is just grinding me down to a nub and there'll be nothing left of me."

We were quiet for a while. The ice felt so good. All I had to do was lie there. Bobby massaged my calves and hamstrings and nobody spoke for five minutes. Then Bobby said, "The tennis tour is brutal. You get December off, then it's an eleven-month season. Eleven straight months of pounding, hours a day, every day, tournament after tournament. Throw in a few flights, sometimes to Australia and around Europe."

I hadn't even done international travel for tournaments yet. "Brutal."

"If a player could stay sharp with his game, not walk away from tournament conditioning, physically and mentally, but magically recover as though he's had a month off, that would be a huge advantage."

"Of course," I said.

"You know what that sounds like, Anton?"

"What?"

"The Tour de France."

"What do you mean? Doping?"

He said, "Given the schedule in the modern era of tennis, it is the most natural fit of all the sports for performance-enhancing drugs."

"Tennis," I said, not believing this. Dad had never mentioned steroids to me and Dad does his research and uses any and all advantage. He would have told me. Then it occurred to me that this conversation with Bobby was sanctioned by Dad.

"Of course tennis, Anton." He stopped massaging my legs and walked to the side of the table so we could see each other. "Look around the sport. There was a clinic in Spain that got busted for PEDs to the Spanish cycling team. They had a file on Nadal. On Ferrer too. Those files were burned later, by the way. And Djokovic? Here's a guy who used to have a reputation for running out of gas in the fourth and fifth sets. He would blame it on a respiratory problem, say he had a problem with glutens. Suddenly he thrives taking matches deep into five sets because he's faster and more fit than anyone. His fellow countryman had a positive test. These guys from the same country are all with the same trainers, doctors. It's pervasive in tennis and has been for years."

I was believing this now. It seemed so obvious in a flash. Getting the simple answer to the riddle that had eluded me.

Bobby said, "Andy Murray? He started flexing his biceps on the court after big points as though he'd never had a muscle before and can't believe it himself. That was not subtle. Did you see Agassi win the Australian in 2003? Whenever does the old guy find the extra guns and extra tank to grind down the young guys? He dismantled people that year. He should have tanked a few games to make it look less obvious."

I was moving from surprise to disappointment and anger. "Is everyone on it?"

"Maybe a few exceptions. A six-ten guy like Isner, that's like serving out a second-story window. Or James Blake, naturally fast as hell. Both those guys never thought they were going pro. They finished high school, just looking to get some college scholarship money. And maybe not Federer. I'm not sure about Fed. Aside from that? Yes. Everyone. Everyone who can afford it and who has the potential to take it and break through to the top."

"You have information on people?"

"Do a web search on the phrase 'tennis has a steroid problem.' A site will come up that collects all the information. Players deny it, of course."

"Okay."

"It's a small community of professionals in this business. I worked in baseball a lot of years. In my opinion, tennis players need the leg up much more than baseball players, but there are far fewer players in tennis with enough money to get on a Cadillac program. Lots more money in baseball. So lots more steroids."

"Jesus Christ." I was a babe. Not yet eighteen. People around me were taking life-altering drugs to make a career, for world fame and millions of dollars. If I were still in school, I'd be studying for a history test, trying to figure out how to get a girl to take her pants off for me. Real kid problems. Not this.

"Sorry to tell it all to you this way, Anton. You're going pro. It's a conversation we knew was coming sooner or later."

"Who's we?"

"Gabe," he said. "Your dad."

I was too weak to nod. I just closed my eyes and lay motionless.

Bobby put his hand on my head. It was gentle. Surprisingly so, the way a bear is surprisingly gentle with cubs. I looked over at him in his too-small T-shirt, hair in a ponytail and his tan, meaty hand. He said, "It's a sort of running joke in tennis that at the end of these tournaments it should be the doctor up on the podium, not the player. Which doctor came up with the best cocktail of recovery drugs."

"I hadn't heard that one," I said.

"Yeah. Not such a good joke, I guess. Anyway, I know most of these guys. These doctors. Think about it." He patted my head a couple times.

"My dad wants me to think about it? Gabe?"

He waited a moment to answer. "They do." He sounded like a guilty man. "I'm sorry, Anton. It's the way it is. All of life is a trade-off. You get to be famous, see the world, get the girls, make lots of money. But you have to put some crap in your body." He took his hand back. "Not a terrible trade, really."

CHAPTER

16

D ad kept on smacking the side of his wineglass with a fork
long after the room had gone quiet. We were at a birthday
dinner for Mom with our family and a dozen friends at Merion
Cricket Club. The party was on the porch dining room overlook-
ing the great lawn that was used for grass tennis and sometimes
cricket matches. Built in the late 1800s, the club looked like an
English country estate. Little had changed since the time umbrellas
were called parasols and the members arrived by horse and carriage.

When Dad was certain all eyes were on him and there had been
plenty of time for dramatic effect, he rose up above us and lifted his
palms like an evangelical. "Welcome," he said. He and Mom were
one table over from Panos and me.

Everyone murmured something in response.

"What a day," he said. "What a day." More pause. More effect.
He could have been one of the great dictators. It's as though he studied old footage of Mussolini, making a short declarative statement

then the silent, affirmative head nods as he scanned the audience back and forth, bathing in the triumph of the words. "My beautiful wife is fifty today." He turned to her. "More beautiful today than ever." He cupped his hand over her ear and the side of her head. "We've had such a beautiful life, such magic together."

"Oh, barf," said Panos in my ear.

I had to stare at my lap. Panos kept watching because he wasn't close to laughter. He really was nauseated. Dad always made these over-the-top toasts that were total bullshit. No connection to anything that we are. It was plausible that he and Mom were negotiating a divorce settlement on the drive over and he'd have made the same toast. No matter what traumas or toxic events were happening in our lives, the toast cleared it away for him. So let it be toasted, so let it be written, so let it be real. If never mentioned by him, then it wasn't official, not even acknowledged and didn't count as a part of our family history. He dialed it up ten times more when people other than family were around.

I know his actual words were fine and I sound cynical, but you never had to live with him.

The toast went on too long and when it was over Panos said, "Let's get a drink at the bar."

Nobody ever checked ID at the club, especially when parents were around. We gave Mom and Dad a wink and a wave, two brothers off to do wholesome, brotherly things. They smiled back and we walked to the Cricket Bar, dim with a low fire, dark wood panels, dark carpets, soft lighting. It felt like the quarters on a ship of a nineteenth-century monarch. The bar was empty except for the bartender so we sat and got two beers.

"When do you leave for the ski trip?" I said to Panos.

"The twenty-second," he said.

I nodded, said nothing.

"Wish you could come," he said.

There was no prohibitive reason. Except Dad. Panos got to go to high school, go to college, take ski trips where he might twist his knee or bruise his shoulder. He even got to play tennis. He played doubles on his college team, one of the kids I might have hustled for $500 five years earlier. He went to Pepperdine, a gorgeous college campus in California, far from Main Line Philadelphia. "Me too," I said.

"You're knocking on the door now, Anton. All the work you put in, even if it doesn't turn into something big, it's an experience you have that you can tuck away and you're still a teenager. But it looks like it's going to turn into something."

"It's going alright," I said. I wondered if Panos knew anything about the steroids. I hadn't yet taken any at that time. I was still in the period of thinking it over. It was like standing on the edge of the thirty-foot high dive and feeling there was no way to will myself over. I sipped my beer which tasted like crap to me as all alcohol did then and I said to Panos, "Did you know Dad wants me to start taking stuff? Performance-enhancing drugs?"

Panos didn't look at me and didn't say anything so I knew the answer before he said it and thank God he was honest. "I know."

We were both silent, looking straight ahead.

We went on like that for a while until Panos said, "We could take off."

"Take off?" I said.

"Sure."

"What does that mean?"

"I don't know exactly, but leave. We've got the money, we'll get you tickets for the ski trip for starters. Then come live with me at college. At least for a while."

"You're nuts."

"No, we could." He was excited and turned his stool to face me. "You can call home from a blocked number, they'll know you're fine, won't call the cops. You can say you need time out and you're taking it."

I laughed.

"Anton, I'm serious."

"Hey, I'd love to go skiing for a week."

"Then come live with me at school. College with no classes. And I'll cover for you with Mom and Dad. Tell them we've been in touch but I don't know where you are."

"I suppose it could work."

"It could work for a while," he said. "It could give you a break."

It already felt good just talking about it. I felt empowered discussing it like a real option. I remembered sneaking away with Panos as a kid when my young perspective turned a small adventure into a whole world. When I was eight or nine, Dad had screamed at me in frustration that I was giving a lazy practice session and not moving my feet, then he stormed off our home court. Panos sneaked on the court and helped me move the tennis ball machine into the yard where he angled it into the air and shot a hundred balls upward like mortar fire, landing most in the swimming pool in a mock World War Two invasion. One hundred balls were ruined, a small expense for Dad but it was the principle and a major act of defiance, which we paid for, and it was worth it. It was something I knew we'd retell as old men.

I imagined sleeping on the floor of Panos's room after a party with girls and grain alcohol punch. Waking up to get a breakfast of crappy fried cafeteria food then napping off the hangover, exercising once or twice a week but only as a means to liven myself up, like taking a shower. Since Liz, I'd had no one to share moments of imagined rebellion. "I could use a break."

"Of course," he said.

We were quiet for a moment which was a mistake. The silence left room for reality to sneak back in. The momentum we had built wasn't enough to carry even thirty seconds of dead air. "You think it might work?" I said.

"Sure." Much weaker voice than before. I heard the difference. He heard it too. We both knew Dad would stalk us, hunt us down, bring us back to a life worse than before.

"Yeah," I said. We wouldn't do it. That was obvious, but it felt good to be loved for something other than being a tennis player. Panos loved me not as a tennis player, just as a brother who might come live with him in his dorm room.

Quiet again. We'd just been on the same up and down fantasy ride and were catching our breath. Panos said, "What are you going to do? About the drugs?"

"I don't know. They're telling me I can't do it without the drugs. Lately my body is telling me the same thing, but I don't know."

"I'm sorry, brother."

"Thanks, Panos." It would be worse without him.

17

In March I entered the Miami Open where four of the top-ten players in the world were in the draw, including the world's number one player. One of my earliest memories as a toddler was visiting this tournament back when it was called the Sony Ericsson. Spectators, reporters, camera crews moving around a complex of dozens of courts and vendors selling T-shirts, drinks and hot dogs. Now people were coming to watch me and I was playing great against the best. Of course now I was taking the drugs. Nothing with needles. Just oral supplements and I never asked for details about what. Plausible deniability. It was only with a wink and a nod that I knew they were steroids at all. But I knew.

Because it was Miami there was a little more star power in the crowds. Who knew Jay Z liked tennis? That gave us something to talk about.

My first-round match was against the eighth seed who was ranked twenty-two in the world. I pummeled him. My serve was clicking, my ground strokes were heavy and locked in, I was focused, anticipating his shots and moving fast and always forward. He was stunned and shaken after the match. He knew that he didn't just have an off day or that I had a fluke day. He was routed by a better player and that put a new and lower ceiling on his career.

A weaker player had squeaked by to face me in the second round and I beat him in straight sets: two and two. People around the tournament were starting to talk about me. I was an eighteen-year-old up-and-comer. Maybe the future of American tennis. And next up for me at the Miami Open, the world number one. The meat-grinder. Ilya Kovalchuk. 6'1" Russian, lean body, all muscle and bone who moved around the court fast and easy like a design for perpetual motion that never has friction with surfaces. He had a rugged, handsome face and always ruffled hair like a youthful lumberjack, only he had experience. He had been a top-five player in the world for twelve years.

The first thing I noticed when taking the court against Ilya was that there were fifty times more cameras than I'd ever played in front of before. Flashes popped and shutters clicked like a swarm of locusts. There were the big TV kind of cameras pumping the match out to homes around the world. I saw John McEnroe. He looked right at me so I waved. Even in repose he always had this intense furrow in his brow like he was going to serve one up the middle on you. He just nodded back to me and the nod seemed to say, "You're an American. Don't disappoint me."

I took my chair courtside and I wasn't rattled at all. I wanted to get out there and crank my serve up, blow everyone's hair back. I had inhuman, synthetic strength running through me, new muscles I hadn't experienced before, and I was still very impressed with myself.

Against the world number one I had nothing to lose. I took the court and played big and aggressive. I went for my serves, my forehands, even my backhands and they were all landing. I played up by the baseline, dictating points, pushing Ilya back into the fans.

He was feeling around for my weak spots. He'd never played me before, probably hadn't seen much of a scouting report on me so he had to find my weaknesses in real time. He was a more seasoned, smarter match player than I was but his smarts wouldn't matter if he couldn't impose his will.

I kept pounding the ball, ripping low percentage service returns that went in anyway.

He was such a pro. I got a few raised eyebrows from him but he didn't rattle. He was used to lower ranked players going for broke against him. That can win some games but it's hard for those low percentages to survive a whole match. He wanted to keep fighting, keep probing me, wait for the match to settle in.

I took the first set.

At the changeover, he looked up at his player box to his coach. I knew he was thinking, "Who is this kid?" It was the same reaction as my first-round opponent. He wasn't having an off day and I wasn't having a fluke. I was a big, strong, fast player with lots of weapons and I was pushing him around, controlling the match. It wouldn't be enough for him to step it up. He needed something from me. He needed me to take my foot off the gas. This match would be determined by me, not him, and I could see he knew that. It was the first glimmer of concern in his expression.

I started the second set the same way I started the first. The drugs had a beautiful effect on me. I had no soreness and was stronger but that was only half of it. It was also psychological.

My body was an endless well. I could keep scooping out buckets of water and never run dry. That gave me the confidence to go pick a fight because I knew I couldn't be hurt, couldn't get tired, couldn't lose my breath even for a moment no matter how hard I ran. Picking a fight, metaphorically, on the tennis court is a powerful thing. Most fights never actually happen. It's just that one person shows a greater willingness to fight and so then he's the winner.

I broke his serve then held mine to go up 3–0 in the second set. It's a best of three sets match so I was three games from beating this guy. McEnroe might smile, even hug me. This was my match to lose.

And it was that subtle shift in how to think about the moment that changed the match. After all my great play, I had something to lose now. I let him back in. Instead of going for everything, I gave myself a few more inches from the line, bigger margin, better percentages, but he got to my shots just a little bit more easily and rather than just managing to get my shots back, he got them back with purpose, with a plan. Now I was the one lunging, reacting to missiles coming in at angles. He won the second and third sets. Match to the world number one.

I felt great anyway. No win had ever made me feel better than this loss had. For a set and a half I had controlled play with the best player in the world. I had all the pieces, I needed only to put them together and keep them together, then I would dominate the tour.

Dad had seen everything I had felt. He entered me in hard court and clay court tournaments around Europe for the summer. It was time to travel, be a real pro.

Every aspect of the tour required conditioning. I needed to condition myself to life in hotels, to living out of a suitcase for months at a time, to surroundings that slid past me like an Epcot trip around the world.

Looking back these years later, I wish I had done more to experience life then. All those cities, people. I never once went to a museum, a show, an urban park. Weeks at a time in Paris every year and all I ever did was make nonstop trips between the courts and the hotel room where I ate, slept, played PlayStation and read books. The irony was that the farther I got from home as my travel world expanded, the more my professional shell constricted.

My time in foreign cities was spent in an impenetrable bubble, like travelling in the Popemobile, only the bubble wasn't so much to prevent threats to my security but threats to my focus. All of this reinforced my one-dimensional self. It was an opportunity blown.

I would still count paces down hallways to the elevator, stripes in a carpet pattern, the number of French fries on a plate next to my cheeseburger. I'd sit to lunch with Adam and after a period of silence he'd say, "How many, Anton," and I'd laugh then say, "Thirty-four. Thirty-four French fries."

In the early years I didn't socialize much at all with other players. Lots of guys on tour would get together in each other's rooms to play poker, watch movies, play video games. I was socially timid and it didn't help that I was a few years younger than everyone. I just read a lot of books which was something I had in common with absolutely no one else.

I entered a clay court tournament in Spain that was a tune-up for the French Open. I loved to go to the restaurants and hear the foreign language around me, imagine I was Hemingway who would order Spanish wine, drink, smoke, fight and womanize. I was obviously American.

I went to a centuries-old café full of people that bookend the stages of raising a family. The young, hip and independent, and then the very-much-older whose kids were grown and gone so they were independent again and could sit in cafés like Picasso.

The waiter was thin and in his fifties. He came over, humble, almost apologetic for his native tongue and took my order. He wore a starched black shirt, black tie with a white apron over top. Not a student looking for extra income, but a professional waiter, a lover of wine and cigarettes, maybe from a long line of waiters. I loved Spain because it felt old and I wanted to go to the old cafés. This restaurant was older than the city of Atlanta, maybe older than the sport of tennis. I felt better perspective on life in places like that. That was about the extent of my social life on the road.

I was the third match on a stadium court and I went to the players' lounge knowing I had anywhere between two and five hours to wait so I brought a book. *White Noise* by DeLillo.

Rufus Parker was an American player ranked below me and we were friendly because all American players get to know each other a bit. "You reading a book?" he said.

He sounded like this all must be a practical joke I was playing on him. "Yes. Got a few hours to kill."

"Jeez. Big brain on Anton. Maybe we should get you a tweed coat and a long, skinny brown cigarette, professor."

Because I'm reading a book? "Rufus, if I knew this would disturb you so much, I would have carried a book out to the court before all our matches."

He laughed. "It is a little disturbing, though. I've been on the tour six years. I haven't read a book in nine. And that was only the first few chapters of *Harry Potter*."

I was seventy-five percent sure he was messing with me. "Serious?"

"Serious."

He was. I laid the book down and stared at him. "No books at all?"

"You're the freak, not me," he said. He looked around. There were seven other players in the lounge. "Let's take a poll," he said. He stood and called across the room. "Raise your hand if you read a book in the last year. An actual book, magazines don't count." Seven blank faces directed at Rufus. "In the last two years?" Blank faces. "In the last five years?" Several smiles, no raised hands.

I knew most of the players personally but not all. I said, "Does everyone here speak English, understand the question?"

Rufus laughed and someone across the room yelled, "Blow me, Anton."

My first thought was, Those poor saps, but I later wondered if there was some benefit to that kind of wiring for this kind of life. If the real goal was happiness, I seemed to be doing worse than most.

Gabe was great in helping me adjust to international play. We'd walk the courts together before tournaments started, while the grounds were empty. He'd walk me to the stadium court and measure the height of the net, walk off the distance from the net to the baseline, examine the right angles of the tape. Everything to show that a court is just a court, no matter where in the world, no matter if they speak French, Spanish or German around you. He'd belabor the obvious until it was funny and relaxing, like Gene Hackman taking his bumpkin Indiana basketball team to a fancy stadium for the first time.

I had craved newness and this was new. My body still seemed

new as well. My strength excited me and my training had become a more pleasant escape. When frustrations and phobias began to swell, I could go to the gym, let the sweat pour, work my muscles with fury, have the physical me drive out the emotional me, grind myself down and burn out the pain. Cauterize my soul.

Endorphins wear off though and the pains in my mind would come back around and I'd train more, and so would go the cycle to keep things at bay, though never cured. The only cure for loneliness is company. I thought maybe a girl might help but what eighteen-year-old girl could drop her school plans to travel the tennis tour so that we could be together more than just December. I still felt so burned by Liz, even years later, that I had no confidence, and that avenue felt closed to me.

My relationship with my shrink, Dr. Ford, was a joke, and he and I both knew it. We did phone consultations biweekly which were useless. Even when we were in the same town we did the session by phone, which pronounced our relationship a joke officially. I never told him about taking steroids. He knew though, and asked me about it, which means he must have been speaking directly to Dad. Probably fucking illegal to do that. I never checked.

Anyway, I was playing well. My best match to that point was still the loss to Ilya at the Miami Open, but I was playing very well that summer leading up to the US Open in August.

CHAPTER

18

The hell you are, Anton. You are not going."

I'd never shopped for clothes for myself before in my life, but that morning I'd gone to Macy's alone. I had no idea what might look good. Much less what a woman would think looks good, but a cute female sales clerk picked out a shirt, pants and shoes for me. Put the whole thing together. It's amazing how nice clothes that fit and aren't for the gym can make you feel different. I was standing in them. "I'm going, Dad. I already told everyone I'm going."

"You are not. Not by a long shot."

"Wrong," I said.

"Don't you realize what this means? What this will do?"

"What, exactly, Dad?"

"It's like spotting three games to your opponent. At the US Open. The US Goddamn Open, which happens in four goddamn days."

"How does having a night out with friends give away three games?"

"A night out? Do I really have to answer that?"

"I'm not going to drink."

"You're damn right you're not because you're going to stay right here." He waved his arm around the Manhattan hotel room that was like every other hotel room I'd stayed in almost every night for the last five months. "Who are these friends, anyway?"

"Rufus. Some other people." I didn't know who all, other than Rufus, but he said it was going to be a cool New York crowd. He grew up in Garden City and knew lots of New York people. "I'm supposed to meet Rufus downstairs in ten minutes."

"Rufus," he said. "Rufus would love to have you spot him three games."

"That's not what's happening."

"Deliberate or not, it's what will happen."

"I said I won't drink and I won't be out late."

"No."

I was in fight mode and I was tournament conditioned. Dad hadn't been my opponent before but I tried not to think about it that way. I needed to win the match. "I'm going."

"I said no."

I squared my shoulders. I was about his height by then and I drew myself up, eye to eye. "Are you physically going to stop me? Wrestle me? Maybe dislocate my shoulder four days before the Open? If so, you better get ready because in two minutes I'm walking out that door to the elevator and going out."

"Anton, this is a bad idea. Terrible."

Movement. He'd gone from denying to advising. I didn't respond but walked to the bathroom and looked in the mirror to fix my shirt and hair. I realized I'd never done that before. My reflection looked so different, groomed with a button-down, collared shirt made by Rag & Bone. Who was this kid in the mirror?

I walked back out past Dad who hadn't moved other than to pivot his feet so he could follow my path like a camera.

I opened the door and tried not to pause but couldn't stop my reflexes, like the flinch when you know a punch is on the way. "Not a drop of alcohol, Anton," he said.

I closed the door and hit the down button for the elevator.

Rufus was waiting in the lobby of the hotel wearing a suit and no tie. The suit was crisp with some shimmery material and fitted to him exactly. He looked like the actors that walk the Oscars red carpet. You would never call Rufus handsome but he wasn't bad looking in any remarkable way either. He was tall, lanky and a little goofy looking. Just what anyone named Rufus ought to look like.

"I was waiting for the text message that you weren't coming," he said.

I made a fake laugh. Getting out of the apartment was the biggest win of my career so far and I was still coming down from it. "Where are we going?"

"A place in the Meatpacking District." He jerked his thumb like a hitchhiker but in the direction of the hotel bar. "We're not in a rush. Want to get a drink here first?"

I'd been delaying the decision whether to drink or not and didn't expect to need the answer so soon. I decided then that I'd drink but not this close to Dad. "I'm ready to get out of this hotel. Let's get one there."

Rufus stepped out of the hotel, raised a hand to hail a taxi and one pulled right up as though he had it on a string. I thought that made him look cool.

We dropped out of the August heat into the back of the air-conditioned taxi and drove south. "Who's going to be there tonight?" I said.

"My high school buddies. You'll like them."

I realized I didn't know much about Rufus. "You went to a regular high school?"

"Yeah, Garden City publics. I missed a lot of junior and senior years, but had tutors, got through. Graduated."

"That's great."

"The three guys you'll meet tonight just graduated college in the spring. Through everything, since the eighth grade, it's been the four of us. They're my posse."

He had a posse. I'd have liked a posse. "They travel with you?"

"Just local stuff. Anything you can ride a train to."

"You're lucky."

He nodded. He knew. He said, "Hey man, I'm good but you're the super star. The bigger the star, the bigger the sacrifice." He looked at me and realized how unhelpful that was. "Anyway, you'll like these guys, Anton. And they'll like you. You can have some fun on the tour."

The cab pulled in front of a restaurant named Bagatelle. There were some muscley guys in suits working the door and it seemed like the kind of place where people hoped the paparazzi would show so they dressed up the front of the place with a line of actual velvet ropes. Inside at the hostess station was a six-foot-tall skinny beauty who either faked or had an Italian accent. From behind her at a large booth table with banquet seating against the back wall, three guys stood up and called to Rufus and yelled things like Raise the Roof. Two good-looking girls sat with them and waved.

"We're with them."

We walked to the table where everyone hugged Rufus and looked me up and down. The tables were black, the floors were black and white. The clothes people wore were black. There was almost no color in the room except for red roses by the hostess. After they had all hugged and slapped and messed up each other's hair, Rufus put a hand on my shoulder and pushed me in front of him. "This is my buddy, Anton Stratis."

They all looked so happy and together and the girls were so pretty that I felt lonely.

The biggest friend came around the corner of the table to shake my hand. "Of course we know Anton. You took a set off the badass Russian. That was beautiful." He stopped short of messing my hair but he was drunk and while we kept our handshake going he held my shoulder with his other hand and shook my whole body.

I've never thought of myself as needing or seeking praise, but we all naturally like people who like us. What better thing could I have in common with someone than the fact that we're both rooting for Anton Stratis. "Nice to meet you," I said.

"I'm Tony." He turned to the guy next to him. "This is Rick. And the little guy at the end is Andy." They were all dressed like Rufus. Dark suit, bright shirt, no tie. A posse.

"Hey guys," I said. I could feel how stiff I was, but I was getting more comfortable.

Tony said, "And this gorgeous flower here is Amanda. I don't need any handsome Greeks for competition, so don't even think about it." He belly-laughed at himself and waved to the other girl. "This is Cici who is also spoken for, but they have friends on the way."

Amanda smiled and did the ladylike handshake, palm down as though reaching in a cookie jar. Cici waved to me from across the table. They both had blonde kinky hair with Miami tans.

Even though the restaurant was full of people eating dinner, there was club music playing and the DJ by the front door upped the volume. Tony swept Amanda up to the banquet seating to dance. People at other tables got on chairs to dance. It was an Americanized fantasy of Italian nightlife.

On our table was a two-gallon glass bowl of green liquid with eight colorful straws. Rick slid it toward me. "Party Mojito. Price of admission."

Here we go. I was just fitting in and didn't want to hesitate so I leaned in and pulled from a straw and in my imagination heard the scream of Dad's voice, "Are you out of your mind—drinking booze and sharing germs with six idiots four days before the US Open?"

It was syrupy and tart with enough alcohol that I could taste that too. "Thanks." I sat in a chair facing the table with Tony and Amanda dancing across and above.

Andy, the runt of the pack, sat next to me. "What was it like going up against Kovalchuk?"

"Hard," I said. I realized I'd never talked about that match socially, only in a press conference when I measured what I said, made sure I was a good sport. "He just keeps coming at you."

"He's a machine," said Andy.

"He's tough. Very tough mentally," I said. "I think my best game is better than his best game, though. I could have won that day if I just stopped thinking and played." I'd never said that out loud before. I hoped it didn't sound cocky.

"That was obvious to anyone watching," he said. "I don't mean about the thinking part or you faltering. Just about who can elevate their game to a higher level. You're going to be the number one player in the world one day."

Compliments from strangers could boost my spirits. It was right in this moment of feeling great and accepted that over my right shoulder I had a glimpse of a stunning brunette woman. She was visiting from another realm, superimposed on the room, like the character in science fiction who can still walk around when time is stopped and pluck things from the fingers of frozen people and re-arrange everything before time starts again.

Her face reminded me of Audrey Hepburn only less fragile, lips more full, facial features elegant but with the bold and broad cheek bones more like a Chinese woman, her body more athletic, built for the modern age. I turned in my chair to have a full frontal gawk. Just as I had her square in my sights, Amanda screamed behind me and I rotated back around. Amanda was in a deep knee bend on the banquet seating, one hand to her face and the other pointing across the restaurant. "Ana!"

By the time I turned back around to Ana, she was on top of us. She stopped right in front of me. "You must be Anton."

Holy crap. "Yes." I put my hand out, fast, like I'd seen something flying at me at the last moment. She took my hand in a grip. My brain was stimulated to the point that it recorded very little. I stood up in the middle of the handshake.

She was about 5'4" and her eyes followed me. "You just keep going up and up," she said.

"Hi, yes, sorry about that."

She was with another girl, the poor thing. Practically invisible next to Ana. The two women walked to the side of the table by

Amanda who had stepped down to ground level and the three of them hugged then said hellos to the rest of our group.

I dropped back into my seat where Andy was still waiting by me. "Kovalchuk is a beast, but you have more raw talent. It's like Lendl and McEnroe. Lendl ruined tennis, especially for guys like Rufus. If everyone partied like Rufus, level playing field, he'd be ranked twenty spots better."

I looked at Rufus who was taking a long pull off the Party Mojito. Maybe Dad had a point. "That may be true," I said.

"Lendl ruined modern tennis. He started training so hard, then winning. Vitas Gerulaitis wasn't made to play tennis that way. Vitas was made to be either a rock star or a tennis player in the pre-Lendl era. Rufus can't compete like this either. He might hold his ranking a couple more years but he's pretty much peaked. It's too bad. Tennis weeds out some of the greats just because it's too grueling, same way people don't want to run for president because it's such a nightmare to campaign."

I looked over at Rufus who was standing with a waiter now, ordering lots of food to the table and dancing while he did it. The restaurant was filling up and feeling more like a nightclub. The DJ raised the volume again so the patrons raised their voices and conversations had a maximum distance of three feet.

Andy knew a hell of a lot about tennis. He could go on. I was an oddity for him. I was just a young kid, someone he could put an arm around, give advice, act paternal with. But he was in awe of me. He loved tennis and I was a tennis god to him.

Food came to the table family-style and most people sampled things while standing and dancing to the DJ. I sat and talked a little and listened a lot to Andy. Rufus kept circulating around but never stopped dancing, even when talking. I sipped the same glass of beer.

"Why so sad?"

Ana was behind me, pulling up a chair. "Not sad. Just not drunk."

"You don't need to be drunk to stand up and dance."

I smiled. No way I was dancing in front of her. "Maybe later."

She sat. "Big match in a few days, I guess."

"Are you going to watch any of the Open?"

"I'll come for one of the early rounds, then I'm going out of town."

"Where to?" She was so beautiful it was impossible to know how old she was.

"New Zealand."

"That's where they make all the movies these days."

"Exactly."

"You're going to make a movie?"

"I am."

I should have known who she was but she didn't mind. She was amused. Truly. She wasn't miffed or pretending amusement. "Have you been in other movies that I would know?"

"You might know some, but I'm pretty new to this. I played Bradley Cooper's daughter in *Hell's Kitchen* that came out last year. Small part. I have a bigger part in a Sam Mendes film that comes out this fall."

"Great."

I didn't know who Sam Mendes was which must have been apparent because she said, "He's a director." She smiled. Charming, and again not miffed. She found my cluelessness about her and her industry to be refreshing. I could relate to that.

"You know anything about tennis?" I said.

"I like to watch it on TV sometimes. That's about it."

It felt safe to know so little about each other. "That's how I feel about movies."

She laughed. "I hear you're pretty good but I've never seen you play."

"How do you know Rufus?" This question was loaded. I was very interested in this girl and starting to feel less awkward. I was having a real conversation. With a girl. In a restaurant. Drinks on the table. The whole situation felt impossible, like I was playing out a scene alone in my bathroom mirror. I kept pretending, trying to fake bravado.

"We met only a couple times. I'm friends with Amanda who's dating Tony. She did publicity for the Bradley Cooper movie and we've been friends since."

"How long will you be in New Zealand?"

"Nine months. Maybe more."

Damn. She'll probably be naked on a beach with a co-star by month three. "Do you mind if I ask how old you are?"

"How old do you think?"

I was young but old enough to know this could be troublesome. Thirty seconds alone with Wikipedia could have gotten me out of the jam. I decided honesty was best. "How old you look and how old you seem are two different things."

"Okay."

"You look twenty. You seem maybe twenty-five. In a good way. Together, poised."

"Eighteen."

Eighteen. Just like me. This was meant to be. I had just finished *Love in the Time of Cholera*. I felt like the poor, young boy who met the only girl he'd ever love but couldn't be with her, so decided he'd do whatever it took, wait however long. There was a fate connecting these characters in fiction, there was a fate connecting Ana and me. A fate as strong as my fate with tennis, both planned for me long before I was born. Or so I hoped in that moment. "Me too," I said.

She smiled. She had this big, booming smile like Rachel McAdams. The kind that had spirit and must come from the inside. There was so much understanding in that sweet, beautiful smile. "Young," she said. "For all this." She nodded her head to our table but kept her eyes on me.

"You must be a good person," I said.

"Oh?"

"You can't be a bad person and have a smile like that." I believed that and so I didn't think it came across as a line. "How old were you when you started acting?"

"Serious acting has been only three or four years. I gave up regular school for tutors about a year ago. I'll go back to school, to college at some point. In some way." She wasn't defensive but she was still making peace with these decisions.

"And your parents? They want you to act or stay in school?"

"They left it up to me."

"Really? That's fantastic."

I sat straighter in my chair. She laughed. I was embarrassed at how elated I was for her. "I heard from Rufus you have a different situation."

"I do." It never occurred to me until that moment that other players had a perception of me and my family that could be discussed around the tour. "What did he say?"

"How shall I put it? You have a very involved father."

"Mmm. Correct."

She sipped her drink. "People express love in lots of different ways."

I sipped my beer because I'd seen her do it and it gave me a moment. "Who do you talk with?"

"What do you mean?"

"A conversation like this. Who is usually on the other side?"

"Well, it's not always the same person."

"Isn't that hard, though? To have it be a rotation? They need to know you."

"They do, at least at the time of the conversation. I had good friends in middle school, ninth grade. I see them less now, but, you know, I see other people."

"Work people?"

"Sure."

"Friends?"

"A few."

I nodded. I didn't want any more beer.

"And I see someone. You know. A psychiatrist."

I perked up again. "Yeah?"

She misinterpreted my interest as fascination with the concept of therapy but I was only happy for another piece of common ground. "He's more like a friend with no other connections. A smart source of advice. I'm not in crisis and they say that's the best time to be in therapy."

"Sure, yeah," I said. "I see someone too. He sucks though."

She sat forward with concern. "Why do you say that?"

"He's another drug my dad wants to put me on to get me to play better." I knew this sounded plaintive and juvenile.

I wanted to rephrase but she let me off the hook anyway. She looked more concerned and a little confused.

"What I mean is, the guy's not fixing me, he's just fixing me up to get me back on the court. We're never talking at a level where the possibility of not playing tennis is on the table."

"That's bullshit." She was mad. She cared. I liked that.

"He's paid by my dad to help my tennis."

"That's not helping you. That's abusing you. They can't mess with you like that."

I shrugged. "Too late."

She took her purse off the table and pulled out a pen, then wrote on a cocktail napkin. She handed the napkin to me. "I don't want to interfere. This is the name of the guy I see and he's great and if you ever want to try something else, I think he'd be good for you."

I put the napkin in my pocket. Something from her. A physical connection now that we would share forever and I'd keep it with me, on me, always, even during matches I'd put it in a plastic zip-lock bag in my pocket so I wouldn't sweat through it. "Thank you."

She nodded. "You should call him, Anton."

The second time she said my name. "Do you read books much?" I said.

"All the time."

"I want to send you one."

"Which book?"

"I'll surprise you. It'll be something to read in New Zealand."

"Good," she said.

I had the social experience of a four-year-old but I could tell she liked me. I knew. Even a four-year-old can know.

She said, "I'll email you my address when I get there."

Four days later I won my opening-round match. Two days after that I woke at 7am to a high-carbohydrate breakfast. Two plates of french toast and cut fruit. I was the third match in the daytime schedule on Arthur Ashe, after a mixed doubles match and a women's singles, so I'd probably get on around 2:30pm.

I met with Gabe then stretched with Bobby and was getting dressed to have a light practice round at the tennis center at noon when my phone beeped with a text message.

good luck in your match today!! ana

Euphoria started in my chest and moved to every molecule. She would have had to ask Rufus for my phone number.

I texted back.

thanks. u coming out today?

And back from her.

> just got to seats. with a mimosa

The more famously underage a person, the less anyone checked ID. I tried to think of something funny to write back. *Don't get too drunk and yell during my service.* No, obnoxious. *Wear sunscreen, it's a hot one.* Pathetic. *I'll play my best for you.* Loser. *Meet me in the locker room after, maybe we can shower off together.* Wow, that one just popped in there. I wrote:

> i'll look for you

She wrote back.

> in the nike suite

This was great. Real contact. Not exactly flirtation, but it was too early for that anyway.

Another beep from her.

> will take off one article of clothing for each set you win

Boom. Euphoria, times ten.

> how many do you have on now?

Beep.

7 but i'm keeping the shoes so
5 available

It was a three of five sets match. Time to get to work.

Leaving for stadium now

Gabe was staring at me while my hands shook with the phone. I didn't know if this was a great motivator or a terrible distraction. "What's up, Anton?"

"Nothing. Girl I met."

Gabe dropped it, thank God. I knew he'd pick it up with Dad later.

We took the Mercedes to the tennis center and walked right to the practice courts. I would sometimes practice with other guys on tour. Sometimes Rufus, sometimes with guys that Gabe would arrange for because they had a playing style that Gabe thought I should see. But on match days I always hit with Gabe. It was a good routine to settle me and Gabe was still a solid player and a great rally partner.

My heart rate was up before I took the court so my muscles responded to the already elevated pace of the rest of me. I was ripping shots past Gabe.

"Easy, Anton. Let's take it slow, work the drills."

"Sorry, just feels good today."

"Keep the beast in the cage another couple hours."

Daytime matches at the Open can be brutal. August in New

York. That day was sunny and ninety degrees so it was a hard day even to spectate a match without shade.

I was up against the twenty-eighth seed, older guy, smart, steady, no big firepower. The stadium was about two-thirds full, normal for a hot day, early round match with middle seeds playing. The heat had sedated everyone so when we took the court there was almost no applause to greet us. I looked for the Nike swoosh at suite level.

I tried to find it with a series of looks that covered about a tenth of the stadium at a time. I'd get a towel from one of the kids on the court, wipe my forearms and look around.

Found it. My vision was always good, better than twenty/twenty. I saw that she had been watching me try to find her. Big smile, waving. I smiled unconsciously and waved only semi-consciously. Gabe would have seen it and wondered what the hell was going on. Ana tipped a baseball cap to me. Article number one.

I served first and pinned three aces in a row past the guy. He was the higher seed but he knew who I was and that if my game was on I could beat anyone. He looked to his player box with an expression that said please don't let this be one of those days for the kid.

I kept up the pace and blew him out in the first set, 6–1. At the changeover I looked to the Nike box and pointed my tennis racket at her. She took off her baseball cap and flung it like a Frisbee to the seats in front of her then stood clapping. I did a short bow. This was the most fun I'd ever had playing tennis.

I rolled in the second set, winning 6–2. It was an even number of games so there was no changeover. I walked to the back of the court to get a towel and pointed my racket to her suite again. She took off her spaghetti-strap tank top. Underneath was a blue sports bra. Her stomach was tan and trim. I could see her little belly button. I had the vivid image of rubbing sunscreen over her. She folded the tank top into a ball and threw it from the Nike suite. I bowed again.

People noticed Ana and I were having an exchange. For all I knew Darren Cahill was remarking on it to the ESPN television audience. What I didn't see because I had stopped paying as much attention to the actual match was that my opponent also noticed and was pissed. He didn't want to be a prop in my show.

I could feel him seething from across the net. He was scrambling hard, ripping his strokes with anger, desperate on every point. I hadn't been thinking about putting my foot down on his neck, closing the third and final set decisively. I had been thinking about belly buttons.

There's momentum in matches and ninety-nine percent of the time, momentum in tennis works the same way as momentum for things with actual mass. A reversal doesn't happen immediately. It slows then stops, then picks up speed in a new direction. I was down 5–2, trying to stay in the third set. He won it 6–3.

The crowd wanted to see more tennis so they were fine with me dropping the third, but when I went down 1–3 in the fourth, they got on my side and got loud.

I was the eighteen-year-old future of tennis having his breakout year. I had pushed Kovalchuk to the brink only months before. And I was an American. Playing in the US Open. In New York Fucking City.

It was my serve, down 1–3 in the fourth. Behind my baseline I got a towel and looked over the tennis balls. The fans sensed I was falling out of the match and a chant started in the crowd. One side of the stadium yelled "Anton" then the other half responded "Stratis."

And back and forth it went, from side to side, like a tennis rally. I looked up, around the stadium, realizing the noise was for me, thousands of people trying to pick me up, dust me off, put some fight in me. I wanted to show gratitude so I whipped the towel like a lasso, the way I'd seen in old clips of Steelers fans in the 70s.

I kept doing this while walking up to the baseline and the chant erupted into a frenzy of indecipherable screams. Every fan was standing, yelling, pumping fists. Nobody noticed the weather anymore. The hotter the better. The umpire called for quiet. I slammed an ace up the middle and the crowd yelled louder than before. They realized they had actual power, that if they worked hard enough, they could affect the match.

One percent of the time momentum can reverse with zero gravity. I won the fourth set 6–3. The crowd saved me. I loved New York.

I was so relieved at rescuing a win that I didn't make any motion to the Nike suite. I also wanted to shake hands with my opponent and not clown around. When I took my seat courtside, I drank water and made a more subtle point to the suite with my racket. She laughed and clapped harder, but no shorts or sports bra came flying out.

In the post-match presser, one reporter asked if I was in a relationship with Ana Stokke. As a reflex I said we're just friends. It was a question about my life, not my tennis. It was the first time I felt like a celebrity. A mini one, anyway.

After media and a shower, I dressed and took a moment to myself in the locker room. No messages on my phone from Ana so I typed one.

what happened to article 3?

She typed right back.

that comes later ☺

I stared at my phone, reading and rereading. Good answer. I pressed the button to make this a phone call and she picked right up.

"Congratulations. Great match. I've never had so much fun at the Open."

"Thanks for coming out. It was nice to have a familiar face in the crowd."

"I didn't distract you?"

"Only a little. It was good."

"You were fun to watch. You looked hot out there. Meaning good."

Could talking to girls really be this easy? What have I been missing? "Want to meet for dinner in the city tonight?"

"Oh, I would love to but I can't. I have a ton of stuff to do. I fly to New Zealand first thing tomorrow."

Crap. "Nine months?" I imagined punters in football jerseys running around New Zealand.

"Yeah."

I wondered how far she'd be from Australia. I'd be there in January. "Maybe we'll manage to see each other before too long."

"That would be nice."

I could feel it all slipping away. I was back to being the boy from *Love in the Time of Cholera*. She was being taken away from me, from our fate. "Ana?"

"Yes?"

"I just have this feeling."

"Yeah?"

"Like a gypsy read my palm and told me we're supposed to be together." Strong stuff. Or stupid stuff, not sure.

"Oh, that's so sweet, Anton."

Her tone sounded like a college girl who's been asked to a high school prom. Maybe I was only paranoid. This was the first time since Liz I'd ever verbalized affection for a girl and I had no idea what was happening and didn't trust my instincts about anyone, especially the instinct that said things are okay. I expected at least some measure of reciprocity. "Well, I hope you have a good flight," I said.

"Send me the book."

"I will."

I hung up. This was the same gypsy who knew I'd play tennis.

Which books could I send her? Definitely *Love in the Time of Cholera*. Great love story in the end, really. I could add *Portnoy's Complaint*. Too dark, though. Basically porn. I'd have liked her to send it to me but I couldn't send it to her. *The Bluest Eye* by Toni Morrison? Pretty dark too but good for a girl trying to fit in, maybe.

"Atom Bomb." It was Adam. He was getting all the rackets together for my next round. "Great match, my man."

"Thanks." Maybe I could talk to Adam about Ana. He might understand. I hoped so. I missed Panos, off having a full life in college. Adam was my only choice.

"Back to the hotel?" he said.

"Want to meet for dinner tonight?" I said for the second time in five minutes.

"Sure. And some PlayStation."

"Of course."

In the next round I lost to the fifth seed. It was a grinding five-set match. I didn't play my best or my worst.

The new rankings were published after the tournament. I was number thirty-two in the world.

20

I had a good hard court season that fall and the press coverage on me was positive. The analysts seemed to like me, think I was a good kid, good for the game. My play was compared to Patrick Rafter. Tall but with a low center of gravity, can serve and volley, speed to cover the court.

I loved Rafter's game but mine was never as pretty as his. Like I said, I was more like Safin, more power than finesse. Safin was still a favorable comparison for me. He was a great player but the career numbers don't show how great he really was. He was able to stay focused on professional tennis for only a short window of time.

I would serve and volley about as often as any player on the tour at that time, which wasn't much. The game changed in the years before I was born. The change was partly due to better technology for the rackets, but even more it was due to better technology for the strings. Strings that could grip a tennis ball so that you could rip a swing with everything you had and put deadly spin on the ball. Gustavo Kuerten had the strings before anyone and won three French Opens before other players caught on.

These days a player can out-strategize and out-execute a player like Rafa in a point, drive him way off the court, then Rafa from horrible position can rip a ball for a winner and take the point. Bullshit, really. In the old days, equipment didn't allow that kind of firepower. The game wasn't about "the shot." It was about all the shots before "the shot." Working a point. Some thinking.

If tennis never allowed changes in technology, if the game never left wood rackets and gut strings, then McEnroe would have gone down as the best ever. He was the best at the old tennis, but technology caught him midcareer.

The greatest athletes do fine with the old or the new technology. Sampras would have won majors in the woody era too. Now we have guys on the tour built specifically for the new era and they wouldn't have won a match thirty-five years ago.

I'd do all right in either generation but I prefer the old one because they didn't train so much and winning certainly didn't require drugs.

I called Ana's psychiatrist. His name was Peter Minkoff. Our first session was telephonic because I was at a hard court tournament in Croatia.

"Ana speaks very highly of you," I said.

"That's kind of her. How are things in Croatia?"

I would have been happy to talk more about Ana. "Going well. I'm in the finals tomorrow. I'm playing well. Feeling healthy."

"Your father is there?"

"Yeah, it's the same group, always. My dad, Gabe, Bobby and Adam."

"Mmm-hmm," he said. It was quiet for a while.

I said, just to be saying something, "So it's the same."

"Right. And I assume that while you may not be looking to break routine entirely, you're at least looking to change it, or inject something new into it. If you could wave a wand, pick a few things, where would you start? As an exercise, may I ask you to name three things right now that you would change?"

Specific things I would change. Hmm. Amazingly, I hadn't done this before, and I didn't know where to begin. "Doctor, have you seen the movie *The King's Speech*?"

"Yes."

"There's a scene where Geoffrey Rush is playing the therapist trying to help the king and he says to the king, 'That's what friends are for.' You remember what the king said back to him?"

"No."

"The king said, 'I wouldn't know.' "

"I remember now."

"That's a lot how I feel. I don't have a place to turn that isn't a person on my payroll. I don't have a history of friendships. I don't even know how they work."

"So where would you begin?"

"That's just it," I said. "The problem isn't just about adding something to my routine. It's way bigger. I have no real relationships and that's not fixed by tweaking my schedule."

"That's awfully defeatist for a tennis champion. I don't mean tweaking your schedule. Of course you can make friends by making different decisions in your life."

Silence. Maybe a full minute.

He said, "How did you meet Ana?"

"I had to go to war with Dad just so I could go out to a restaurant for three hours. I met her there."

"Sounds like a new routine."

"It was a one-off."

"Make it more."

"Doc, I'm in a new city every two weeks."

"You have friends on the tour? Players near your age?"

"Sort of. A couple."

"Anton, I'm not saying this is an add-water-have-friends type of thing. I'm saying you have to open yourself up to it. Clearly you want relationships, so be open to the small ways that will help you make friends. It could be the little choices of sitting at an empty table for lunch or the table with two people already sitting. Think about those choices when they come to you."

"Ana's still got months in New Zealand," I blurted out. With busy schedules and different time zones we almost never talked but emailed and texted a lot and usually got back to each other within twenty-four hours.

"Yes, I believe so."

"I told her I thought it was fate that we would be together."

"Mmm-hmm."

"Stupid."

"You believe in fate?" he said.

"I'm not sure. I've never thought about taking a firm position on fate. It's just that sometimes I feel the force of it."

"The force of it."

"Like I'm on a train, on the rails, moving fast. Sometimes it makes me feel good and sometimes not. Sometimes I feel like I'm bracing for impact, inevitable, and I can picture it like it's already played out thousands of times. Actors in a Broadway play that do it all over, night after night." I had my laptop out. I wanted to see the face of Peter Minkoff so I entered the name in a Google search.

"Other times I feel like the train is taking me somewhere good. Somewhere I'm supposed to be."

"That's interesting, Anton. I'm sure every train ride has both some good and bad."

"I suppose so."

"Though I think the analogy breaks down when you talk about the rails. You're not fastened to anything."

He was affiliated with some hospital in New York and there was a photo of him on a page of physician bios. He was late fifties, handsome and kindly, like a less effete Mr. Rogers. I said, "Intellectually, I get that. Emotionally, we have some work to do."

The next day I won the tournament. From the moment of match point there was a tour official on the court for me. Drug test. If I had needed to go to the bathroom before the awards ceremony, he'd have followed me out, kept eyes on me the whole time and taken the pee.

I stayed on court for the ceremony though, and afterward the official and I walked off together. He was discreet, standing by the exit of the court, holding a clipboard, tour credentials around his neck and an official T-shirt. He walked behind me into the locker room where there was another official to meet us.

"Would you like to shower first, Mr. Stratis?"

I knew how that worked. They would stand right in front of the shower, curtain open, staring in, still holding the clipboard. "No, thanks."

If I couldn't pee, he'd give me water and watch me until I could pee. If I got hungry, he'd get me food to eat, but never leave me alone until he got my pee. "This way, then."

We walked to a toilet stall. One official handed me a cup with the cap off and held the stall door open. I peed in the cup, handed it back and they sealed it up. We all signed the paperwork on the clipboard and that was that.

They tested at lots of tournaments. It was random which ones. After a match the loser is tested. If you keep winning, you get the test after the finals. Croatia was my fourth test while on the drugs. Made me so damn nervous.

PART II

maybe . . . the gypsy lied

—Bruce Springsteen

21

I was nineteen years old. Plenty old enough to vote. Plenty old enough to fight. I was at Wimbledon, holding a world ranking near thirty, trying to move up, and Wimbledon was the place where every player wanted it a little more. It had tradition to the point of stuffiness so players simultaneously wanted to be accepted and also to stuff it right back to them by winning their damn tournament.

I'd won three tournaments, smaller ones, but had never gone deep at a major. I was rolling at Wimbledon and rolled right into Kovalchuk in the semifinals, our first meeting since I had pushed him at the Miami Open.

In Miami, the feeling had been electric, the crowd had been with me, my adrenaline surging, and I had put it all to good use, a man possessed.

Wimbledon was different. I was in possession of myself. I didn't go for big, risky shots like a player hoping to pull off an upset. I was calm, even steely, played my regular game the way I'd play it against anyone. The crowd was neutral and hushed the way Wimbledon crowds are. The match was two professionals, focused, lining up against each other in quiet fury.

He beat me in five sets, but I knew he was more afraid of me after that match. When we shook hands at the net I could see that he felt he'd beaten me for the last time, that I would run him down like a racehorse on the last stretch when his ears go flat back and the ground is a blur underneath. Ilya would watch me go by, helpless. I was fourteen years younger. He had to know someone was coming for him.

I didn't think much about getting caught myself then because nineteen-year-olds believe in invincibility and immortality, or at least they aren't conscious of the truth, but eventually someone would have to come defeat me, kill me. Of course they would.

After the match, I saw Mom and Dad for dinner. We went to a restaurant which we never did until the tournament was over for me.

"Anton, how are you feeling, honey? Are you sure you don't want to go back to the room to lie down?"

"I'm fine, Mom."

"Your muscles must be getting tight."

"I'm good."

Dad drank his wine and said, "He could play another five sets right now, dear."

Mom travelled to all the majors, but that's only four tournaments each year so it was uncommon for her to be at the post-match meal. Dad had a near-photographic memory when it came to recounting the match, remembering exactly when certain points happened, even going shot by shot through the point. I guessed it was an expression of love. Getting through the commentary without acting like a disinterested teenage brat was a special challenge.

"Well, we'll get you back to the room early for some rest. Maybe we can watch a movie together?"

"Sure," I said. I ate steak with potatoes and water.

I didn't feel that close to Mom then. I loved her, she loved me, but she took a backseat in my tennis life and tennis was nearly the totality of me. Her role as co-parent, let alone primary parent, ended by the time I was six years old, and I resented her for signing over her place with me so easily. From my perspective, it seemed too easy.

"Do you feel like drama or comedy?" she said.

"Drama," I said. I didn't care, but if I said I didn't care then conversation about which type of movie would go on another ten minutes.

"Oh, good, me too. I looked through the on-demand menu and there are some great ones."

Dad ate. When we weren't talking about tennis at the table, he got his bites in.

If I were one of the millions of kids living in a home below the poverty line, or living in a country where my family, friends and I were on the run from genocidal warriors, then I would understand my unhappiness, could draw a straight line from poverty and genocide to despair.

I looked across to two loving parents dedicated to me, who loved me in their ways. I looked down at a $45 steak. Only a very selfish and bad person would feel less than fortunate. Less than happy.

But a person is happy in his life only if he finds meaning in it, and meaning in life is positively correlated with choice in life. While I wasn't conscious of that fact then, I suffered from it unknowingly.

I clicked through photos of Ana with Ryan Hall walking the red carpet in Los Angeles for the premier of her movie. There were about twenty photos and in most of them his hand was on the lowest part of her lower back. Ryan Hall had a part in the same film but Ana was the star. He had the same agent as Ana and the damned agent kept plopping them in the same films together. Apparently agents did that, Ana had explained to me.

She had told me over the phone about Ryan. Nice guy to work with, good to read lines with, fun to get a drink with while filming in a small-town location, but she never mentioned him as a boyfriend, all evidence in my web browser to the contrary.

I clicked to a photo of Ryan whispering in Ana's ear and maybe taking a nibble while there. She looked happy. I knew they were starting another film together in Vancouver the following week.

I clicked out of the browser and stretched out on the couch to stare at the ceiling. When English or Australian guys on the tour had something bad happen to them, they'd say "I feel gutted." That was how I'd felt with Liz. Clicking through each photo for a lengthy study was the most masochistic thing I'd done and I had a fairly high pain threshold.

Adam walked into the hotel suite and saw me on my back on the couch. I didn't look over.

"What's up, my man?" he said.

"Nothing."

"A little down in the mouth, no?"

"Maybe." I found that I did want to talk about it.

"So what is it?"

"I'm hearing from Ana less and less." Since we met more than a year ago we'd had two dinners and a hundred phone calls.

"She busy on a picture?"

"About to be. It's more that I just looked through some pictures of her snuggling with some actor on a red carpet."

Adam laughed. "You should hear yourself. Really."

"What's that mean?"

"Let me be sure I have it right. You're not getting enough attention from the super-hot-A-list-Oscar-bound actress? You poor thing."

"Screw you, Adam."

"I'm just saying. It's a pretty first-class problem, Anton."

I sat up. Whenever something goes wrong on the court, I need to lead myself back into play with the right attitude, the right body language. I can't win if I don't expect to win. No down-in-the-mouth player wins. "True," I said.

I was in a hole and needed a ladder out. Ana was a twenty-four-carat ladder but I just needed a way up. A wooden ladder would do the job. Any girl. Any friend. Adam said, "Anton, lots of fishies out there. Guy like you? Like a commercial fishing ship. You'll fish out an entire coastline."

"Mmm." The fish-in-the-sea stuff bounced off me. The truth was I didn't want a wooden ladder. I liked Ana.

"So is she dating this guy? They're together?"

"Seems that way, but I don't know."

"Could be just publicity stuff for the picture."

"Yeah," I said.

"It could also be real," he said.

"Right."

"And if it's real, can you blame her?"

I looked at him.

"You two both travel around the planet, maybe rendezvous a few days a few times each year. And you're kids. Legally in bars, you're still kids. For a relationship like that you need to be legally adults. At the least. Probably legally adults plus five years, and maybe a divorce or two thrown in first."

"So no girls until I'm twenty-six."

"Not that. It's just you picked a tough one here. Date someone who's more free to travel with you. Not travel to everything or you'll start to think of her as luggage, but someone who can make it a week each month. Or date a girl on the tour. Half the girl players are your age. Or younger."

Adam was trying to help but the only thing that could help me was to learn as incontrovertible fact that Ana was not sleeping with Ryan Hall. "Yeah."

"Actresses are tough, Atom Bomb. Her star can go up and down, same as yours, and when hers goes down while yours is up, that's hard. Vice versa, hard too. And actresses are insecure. I don't know about Ana, but most of them are. Lots of tennis players date actresses and it never works out. It's been going on since the dawn of the Open Era and that combination always ends ugly."

"She's not insecure." I sounded like a child. I knew it.

"Well, we're not picking a wife now anyway. What you need is a date."

"I don't want a date." I actually did, sort of. I just wanted Ana more.

"Okay, no date." Adam sat down on the chair next to the couch. I thought he was going to turn on the PlayStation but he didn't. "So let's send her a note. A handwritten note."

"I don't have an address for her. Not for a couple more weeks when she's settled."

"Text message it is. Hand me your phone. You're in no condition."

I handed my phone to him. I said, "I read everything first. Don't start firing things off."

"Okay, let's brainstorm."

"Sure."

"What are you doing for Halloween?" he said.

"I don't know."

"What are you going to dress up as?"

"A tennis player."

"Funny. Seriously."

"Adam, I haven't dressed up for Halloween since I was eight. I never do anything for Halloween."

"I'm taking you to a great Halloween party this year." Adam started typing on my phone then handed it back to me and said, "Send this."

It read:

> be my pumpkin, pumpkin

"Jesus." I deleted it before either of us accidentally hit send.

"Come on. That was perfect. Gets the point across, but not too heavy. Still funny and charming."

"It would sound weird. We've never texted like that."

"So change it up. If she's canoodling on the red carpet with another guy, you need to change it up. That's just basic math."

"No pumpkins."

"Fine," he said.

I had an idea. I typed:

> whatever happened to that blue sports bra? article #3

I hit send before reason could get in the way.

"Atom Bomb. What did you write?"

"I have no idea," I said. I held the phone and in my mind listened to the beep from hers. Then mine beeped.

> Still have it. who says the bra was going to be #3 anyway. i had a hot thong that day

Reversal of emotional fortunes. I was sweating, my heart racing.

> it matched the shoes?

Mine beeped.

> a lady is always prepared

I reconsidered Adam's pumpkin message, then wrote instead:

> halloween plans?

> stuck in vancouver. you?

> berlin

> good luck. on the way to dinner! ☺

I leaned back in the couch and the rush subsided. I tossed the phone to Adam.

"Not a bad back and forth," he said after reading.

"I'm in the same spot. She didn't say she's getting dinner with Ryan Hall but she may as well have."

Adam moved next to me on the couch and put an arm around my shoulders. "Buddy, will you let me set you up on a date?"

"I don't know, Adam. I'm an idiot. I wouldn't know what to do on a date."

"You were just talking about thongs with the hottest actress on the planet. That puts you in the top one percent of one percent of people who know what to do." He shook my shoulders. "Come on. There's that hot Croatian. Victoria Jancovic. She's eighteen, mile-long legs."

"Her English is pretty broken."

"Even better. Focus on the legs."

"What, like a dinner?"

"Sure. Or you can even start with hitting practice balls one afternoon. Gabe can set that up."

"Maybe."

"Plus, the media might get a hold of it. Take a few photos. Then it's Ana clicking around the Internet and getting all worked up."

Now you're talking. "Okay, set it up."

"My man," he said.

I had underestimated Adam to that point. Not his strategic capability. It didn't matter what the strategy was. It was that he cared, he was rooting for me, not as a player but as a person. He was getting to know me.

CHAPTER

23

Months later back in New York I saw Dr. Minkoff face-to-face for the first time. I talked for ten minutes about how my life was rote, same routine with the same people in similar hotel rooms with similar tournament results, and an identical me. I could actually feel my utter lack of personal growth.

It was the same talk I'd given him weekly by telephone since he and I started together.

When I had finished, he said, "Anton, now that we're together in person, I feel more comfortable saying this." He paused. "Don't you get tired of hearing yourself?"

I was stunned. He had insulted me. I replayed the remark in my head a few times to be certain, then I was certain that it was a flat insult. "Am I boring you, doctor?"

"We can talk about whatever you want to talk about. I've just noticed that you talk about the same things every time and I wonder if you've noticed as well."

"I have," I said. My voice was clipped and angry.

"Why do you think we're stuck on this issue?"

"Because it's a big issue," I said getting louder. I was in an argument with my shrink.

"It is, and we can make small amounts of progress."

"I was hoping we were."

"We probably are," he said. "But I think we can do more. We can do better."

"Okay." I was trying to cool off, stay constructive, the way I would take a tip from Gabe on the court.

He said, "Before we come up with a plan, we need to determine who the players are, the people who will carry out the plan."

"Sure," I said.

"There's only one that matters, and that person is you, but I'm not sure that you've truly realized that yet."

I wanted to say obviously I have, but maybe there was something not obvious that I had missed.

He said, "You are very recently a child, a dependent, and people, parents usually, made decisions on your behalf. You are no longer a child and you need to enforce that transition in your own life. Given your profession, you have unusual circumstances and I would argue this makes it even more important that you take charge of the way your life is going to be. Only you can set up your life the way you want it. If you offer that role to someone else, if it is usurped by anyone else, then your chance of happiness is greatly diminished."

Our argument had turned into something healthy. Everything he said would have made sense to me at any point in the last years, but now I heard it in such a way that I felt it too. It wasn't just an intellectual thing.

I said, "Sure, I get it. I just don't know how to put any of that into practice. As simple as some of this sounds, it feels very complex."

"Why complex?"

"It's like a two-front war. One front is just to keep moving ahead with my tennis. Then the very support structure to help me with the one front is actually the second front. It's like a virus that makes your cells eat yourself. I need to fight my own team that's helping me fight everyone else. That just feels overwhelming. Depressing."

"I'm sure it's overwhelming to a degree. Not depressing, but it feels big and we'll start to make it smaller."

"No, it's depressing."

"You're not depressed, Anton. If you were truly depressed, we'd look into that and I could prescribe something for you."

"I'm not taking a pill for depression."

He laughed. "That's interesting. Why not?"

"I wouldn't."

"If you felt bad and there was a pill that could make you feel well, why wouldn't you take it?"

Hmm. When he put it that way. "I don't know." It also occurred to me that there was a pill, of sorts, that could make me play well, and I was already taking it.

"You're not depressed," he said again. "You're overwhelmed, daunted, but not depressed."

I shrugged.

He said, "Anton, I've seen many teenagers in my practice, and I've worked with them through their twenties and thirties." He gave me a half smile, the affectionate kind. "You are a highly self-aware young man. Not just for a nineteen-year-old, but for any age."

I watched him and his words swirled around inside me. We watched each other. I smiled. It was the nicest compliment anyone had ever paid me. "Thanks," I said.

"When you leave today, consider yourself at square one. Your naked self with no tennis clothes. Consider that you could be a nineteen-year-old retiree from tennis. What might motivate you then? What would you do?"

"Okay."

"And not just a thought-bubble exercise. Put it on the table. Really make it a choice."

"Okay."

"If you want to quit tennis, let's talk about it. That might be the right answer. If you want to stay with tennis, let's make sure it's for the right reasons and then let's discuss practical ways to improve your life inside and outside tennis. That might mean changing up your team, limiting your father's involvement, moving out of your parents' home and getting your own apartment."

This all sounded good. Dad would hate it.

Y ou cannot make an omelet without cracking eggs. You can- not make a revolution with white gloves. It's going to get worse before it gets better.

I would tell myself things like that over the next couple years. My world ranking hit a plateau at twenty-five but everyone thought I'd be a top-five player by then so everyone was disappointed in me.

I had taken something from my first face-to-face meeting with Dr. Minkoff. I didn't quit tennis, but I quit being the old me. The dependent child. My first step had been to tell Dad that I wanted him to travel with me only to the four majors each year, same as Mom. I knew that would be a fight so I had gone to Gabe first to say that Dad was a distraction to me, that I couldn't focus on tennis and winning in Dad's authoritarian presence. With Gabe on my side, Dad grumbled his agreement. He was off the team.

His departure was like the parent leaving after the drop-off of a college freshman. I had freedoms and free time away from watchful eyes. I hadn't realized how much the constant chaperone my father had become had impeded me from making friends. I spent more of my downtime with other players on the tour, playing cards, watching movies, talking. Drinking.

I dated a few girls on the tour. Nothing serious. No one like Ana, with whom there was little now other than periodic updates that she was happily and casually dating some actor or another.

I was having fun. And having some sex. I'd gone from a nineteen-year-old virgin to a twenty-two-year-old of experience with beautiful women. I was shocked at just how experienced the European women of my own age were. Most had dated older and more experienced European men at some point in their teens and so while I was shocked at the experience they displayed in the bedroom, they were equally shocked at my lack of experience.

But we were all lonely in our ways, and in it together, child campers at a never-ending summer camp. Some of the girls were patient with me, taught me things. By twenty-two, I knew everything that a European pervert twice my age would know.

The worst moments were the frustrated calls from Dad after each loss, threatening to rejoin our travelling band. Nothing useful happened on the calls. He would just ask in a hundred different ways, What's wrong with you? I had no answer to satisfy him so after thirty minutes of mutually inflicted brain damage we would hang up.

This was the two-front war that I kept fighting. The front that was the tennis world, my tennis ranking, was classic trench warfare. I was on one side, the tournaments and hotels on the other, everyone dug in, static, no sign of a breakthrough in either direction.

On the other front, there was movement. It was a campaign

across plains, through valleys and over a mountain pass to liberate the prized, occupied city. For the first time I learned how I handled situations on my own, who was my independent self. Was I funny and goofy on a date to dinner and a movie, or was I brooding and reserved? I didn't have any idea so I tried out different things to see which version of me I liked and wanted to stick with, like picking characters out of a book for me to play.

I hear people say of someone, Oh, he's this type or that type, and Oh, he won't care if you borrow his shirt and I guarantee he won't even notice if you wear it right under his nose. So-and-so is the opposite and would have a conniption.

No one could predict me nor could I predict myself because I had no track record. I felt uncertain, that my behavior would be guided by the moment, that my preferences and will were unformed so that the will of another would drive the moment and I would slot in. That wasn't my nature to slot in. I knew at least that much. I could feel my discomfort. I needed to experiment with enough versions of myself to decide on one of them. It was kindergarten socialization dynamics at twenty-two years old.

It was confusing and frustrating. A sort of rat in a maze, bumping into walls, turning round and round, smelling something he's certain is cheese and trying to get it.

Through the confusion I did feel an undercurrent of progress. I made wrong turns and bumped into dead ends and I was a rat, but I was my own rat.

I remembered reading *David Copperfield* as a teenager and thought again about the opening line: Whether I shall turn out to be the hero of my own life, or whether that station will be held by anybody else . . .

I wondered then what hero meant. What does it take to be the hero of your own life? Choice, certainly. You have to be in charge of your life to be the hero of it. What if you make bad choices, or just-below-average choices? Do you need to reach the cheese to be the hero, and then what the hell is the cheese anyway? Self-understanding? Happiness? A Wimbledon title? Could the cheese be to perform one noble act in an otherwise unremarkable life spent not in charge of it?

In any case, I was taking charge of my own life, setting it up the way I wanted it to be, based on my limited knowledge. I thought that had to be done if I could ever have the opportunity to be the hero.

I would sometimes hum the tune of my metaphor to myself. The dog takes the cat, the cat takes the rat, the rat takes the cheese. The cheese stands alone.

25

I was showered up and back in street clothes after the loss when I walked back into the hotel suite.

"Atom Bomb."

Adam sat in the suite on the sofa next to the PlayStation controls. Gabe was too pissed off to talk with me now. It was a bad loss. "Hey, Adam." There were big windows with a city view but I didn't want a lot of light coming in so I closed the curtains to darken the room.

"Have a seat, my man."

I did and unrolled my whole body into the sofa so that my head rested back and I looked up at the ceiling. The night before I had gone out to dinner with a girl on the tour. We had ordered a bottle of wine. Finished it.

"Tough day out there, Anton."

Before dinner we had visited the Museu Picasso. In my years on the tour this was my first visit to a museum. I was in Barcelona and this seemed like a breakthrough moment, a heroic choice to make in my life. I was in Europe on a date with a pretty girl I liked and so we went to a museum and a fancy restaurant the way many human beings might. "Yes. Very tough day."

Adam slid a PlayStation control to me. "Let's have a round," he said.

I sat up. I looked back at the sofa pillow that held an imprint in the shape of my head as though trying to lure me back. The wine had dehydrated me. It was a hot day for the match and my hydration never caught up. My face had gone tomato red in the first set. I drank water but could never get it all the way to my veins in time. I felt feverish. I was still feverish next to Adam. Our flight out of Spain wasn't until the next morning. "Not now, I can't concentrate. I can barely focus my eyes."

"You feel like talking?"

I did and I didn't. It depended on what Adam talked about. "Sure."

Adam took this word and ran with it. "You seem good to me, Anton. Doing better than in the years I've known you. Sometimes. And then sometimes you're worse."

"I guess so."

"It used to be just you and tennis, man. The two of you pulling on each other, like this linear thing. Now it's not linear. It's three dimensional. Maybe four or five dimensional."

Adam could sound stoned even if he wasn't. I didn't say anything.

"And that's all good, Anton. People need variety, variability. Now your highs are higher and your lows are lower," he said. "The key is to maximize the high and curb the low."

This was the kind of Zen advice I always thought was impractical. "Well, that would be nice." My headache was getting worse. I could feel the beat of my heart in my temples so I massaged them with the tips of my fingers.

"You need some water," said Adam. He handed me a Fiji from a case we kept at room temperature in the suite.

I said, "Four years ago I'd never have gone out to dinner the night before a match, but if I were still living my life that same way I'd be so miserable I'd have quit the tour altogether. Now at least I'm playing. Not as good as a robot, but it's what I can do."

"I know. Believe me, I'm totally with you."

"It's harder to focus. I can get focused, I just can't stay focused and intense for the long haul. There's a lot going on."

"I know, Atom Bomb. It causes mental dislocation."

"Something like that." My face was still red and I still felt feverish. It was partly the dehydration and partly the conversation.

"Your head bothering you?"

"I need Advil."

"That'll help," he said.

Adam stood and walked to his bag hanging from the back of a chair at the suite's dining room table. I rolled back to look at the ceiling again and rubbed my temples.

The suite mini-fridge would hum to life every three minutes or so, marking time with sedated frequency. I looked down at the carpet that had a pattern of blue concentric circles which seemed to my dehydrated brain to move like a cinemagraph. Watercolors of beach scenes each available for €200 were spaced across the beige walls.

Adam returned to stand in front of me with a bottle of pills in each hand. One was Advil. The other was something prescription.

"What the hell is that?"

"Just an idea, my man. This one is Advil." He tossed it in my lap.

"And that one?"

"This one, my friend, has helped me to curb many a low. One pill, no downside, will right the ship."

"What is it?"

"This one," he said again, "is cool water over a hot brain."

"For Christ's sake, Adam. What is it?"

"Valium. Basically, Valium." He tossed that bottle in my lap too. "Serve one pill with one beer, lay down on the sofa, enjoy."

"It doesn't screw me? No hangover or side effect?"

"It'll help you rest, that's all. You need to rest."

I shrugged which he took to mean get me a beer. I took the pill and drank the beer without putting any questions to myself.

We turned on the PlayStation for a while until I didn't want to play anymore. I wanted only to sit back and lower my eyelids by half. Cool water over a hot brain. He was right.

26

I paused in front of my parents' front door. Still my front door, really, since I had only hotel rooms to call my own other than this house.

I knew Dad was home. I knew he'd be pissed. I braced myself, opened the door and walked into the living room where he was seated with his back to me, reading a newspaper.

"Hey, pal."

"Hey, Dad."

He glanced up to me and smiled, then lowered the newspaper. He slowly stood up, the way a person does unconsciously and he turned to face me square. He looked in my eyes, then a few inches higher at my Mohawk haircut. My head was shaved bald on the sides with a three-inch-thick band of hair down the middle, dyed blond. My hair was jet black so I thought making it blond would be an interesting change. "What have you done, Anton?"

"I got a haircut."

"For the love of God, son."

I was ready to defend a punch or shove but he didn't even step toward me. He stepped backward and couldn't seem to catch his breath. "Anton," he said.

"I wanted something different."

"Oh, Anton," he said again. I detected no anger. Disappointment, maybe. Sadness. He kept his eyes on me but felt around behind him for a piece of furniture to support himself. His hand found the sofa and he guided himself in.

"Dad, it's a haircut, it's nothing. Less than a pierced ear." The idea for the Mohawk had come to me in the barber's chair, seemingly out of thin air, but with only a few minutes' hindsight I knew it had come from something real that had been lurking.

"Anton," he said. "I think, maybe," he searched for the words then whispered what he came up with, "I am failing you."

Now my eyes stayed on Dad and in the same unconscious motion he'd had a moment before, my body found the chair behind me. "What are you talking about, Dad?"

"You're so unhappy."

I had told him I was unhappy a thousand times. We had fought about my unhappiness, physically and verbally, through the years but he never grasped or accepted it. What finally reached him was a Mohawk haircut, a minor act of self-mutilation. "Yes," I said.

He began a silent cry. Wet eyes spilling to tears that blurred his view of me. "Anton, I have always been hard on you, of course I know that. Harder than on Panos. But you have a gift." He said the word gift louder, like he was calling to it upstairs.

I said nothing. I'd never seen this from my father before. He was a stranger to me.

His body language changed to defensiveness. A man on trial and he gathered his strength. "I had it different from you. I didn't grow up with millions of dollars and a secure future, options I could just choose from. I had to go get it." He said this with force, trying to relive a moment of conquest. "I had fire in my belly because it's human nature to put fire in the belly when it needs to be there. But what about when it doesn't need to be there? What about you? Your mother and I talked since she was pregnant with Panos about how we would give you kids an edge, some fire. Despite all the comforts and advantages you'd have, how would we make you value effort and goals?"

He was giving me a parenting confessional. Was it an apology? I still said nothing.

"We wanted to give you the fire in the belly that we had growing up. And then you had this gift too. It was obvious early on." He raised his hands to say, come on, anyone could see this gift and would have acted on it. "Did we do everything right? No way, of course not. I know that." He nodded. "We tried our best." He fell silent.

"So you don't like the Mohawk."

He smiled. "No, son."

"Alright," I said.

"Hell, screw the Mohawk, whatever." His smile grew. It was forced, but it got big enough to show teeth. "I'm just worried about you, Anton."

I decided then to abandon the Mohawk. It would take a few weeks but I'd let it grow in. I knew the media would say I'd gotten brash, cocky. They'd say I wanted attention and if I couldn't get it by winning tournaments then I'd get it another way.

They'd be wrong, naturally. It was the opposite. The Mohawk was a costume, not me but a presentation of me, a way for an actor to play me on the court while the real me could hide away.

It was a bad choice, though. Agassi had one, so it wasn't the first. James Blake shaved his head bald, though that was in support of his dad getting chemo treatment. But the Mohawk wasn't me. It was one of the many things I tried on that didn't fit. Even if I wanted to hide, the presentation of me had to fit with me.

I played one tournament with the Mohawk, then I moved on from that haircut more quickly than the media did. There were plenty of articles with photos. I hoped Ana didn't see any of it.

Ben Archer won that tournament. Same haircut he always had, wearing conservative tennis whites. Same steady demeanor and steady game, but with that win he was ranked above me for the first time. I was at twenty-three and he moved up to fourteen.

He was a marvel to me. He seemed so damned normal.

The thing about the Mohawk, though, was that it provoked a piece of Dad that was almost normal too. I didn't see the light or now agree with anything he'd done, but it was the first time I had witnessed something human from him.

CHAPTER

27

I rented a three-bedroom house in Palm Beach Gardens. It was in one of the gated communities that have only two or three architectural plans for the couple hundred houses in the development and most are lived in only during the few months of winter or are rented out year-round to people who come golfing for a week at a time. It was alarmingly un-homey, but big enough for friends to come visit. Miami was known to be the steroid capitol of the world at that time but my choice of home had nothing to do with that fact. Bobby took care of all that. I didn't know and it was better for me that way.

Manhattan would have been fun. Panos was there. He was a financial advisor at J.P. Morgan, managing rich people's money. Managing a small amount of Dad's money and all of my money now that I was a millionaire by myself. He also managed investments for a few tour players he'd met through me and so had started a nice business for himself. But a decent place in Manhattan was a fortune, plus tennis courts were harder to come by. I'd average about forty nights a year in whichever home I picked and I wanted a place where the weather was nice in December. Anyway, most players on the tour lived in the stretch of Florida between Orlando and Miami, so Palm Beach Gardens put me right in the middle.

Dad allowed it. He had backed way off me since the Mohawk, treating me like a rescue dog. He always understood action-reaction but had assumed my reactions to him always resulted in better tennis. Now he saw there were unknowable, unseen reactions that could show up in disturbing ways and that made him feel uncertain and guilty. He was fearful of causing more damage so if I wanted something enough now I could get it.

Gabe took a condo on a golf course in Palm Beach Gardens nearby. We trained on the same schedule as ever, but the air had gone out of both of us. He didn't talk about the top three players in the world anymore and how we'd catch them, or how the draw looked for getting to the second week in the major tournaments. It was more about day-to-day survival, how we'd manage just to keep it going. Keeping it going had become the routine, and we'd both lost sight of where to.

I floated through the tennis season relying on my serve and my steroids to win enough. No leg work. I knew Dad was upset, thought I was wasting good years, and he was right.

"Anton, let's go to beach. For valk and for svim."

I never dated the American players. Almost exclusively Eastern Europeans. Russians in particular because those girls all had childhoods that were way more fucked up than my own. I was semiconscious of the fear I had of dating an American, that I would be the one judged to be more screwed up, to be pitied. That she would have a background of friendships, going to concerts, birthday parties, favorite songs that reminded her of first dates, first kisses, rather than my experience which was nothing at all except an eight-month fraud at the hands of Liz, and then skipped right to sexual instruction from a girl with far more knowledge than I had. "Sure, for an hour maybe. I have a practice session at one o'clock."

So no Americans. I was intimidated. Dr. Minkoff helped me to see that. Anyway, Eastern Europe seems to turn out only girls who are 5'11" with a great ass. "Good, I practice at vun also."

I stood from the bed naked and took an energy bar from a box on the bedside table. Athletes in training eat constantly. I always had food with me and never went more than a single waking hour without eating something. I opened a second energy bar while still standing by the bed.

She grabbed my penis with one hand and pulled me back into bed. "I need bite also."

It was unclear, but turned out she meant the energy bar. She took a bite, then pulled me over top of her and wrapped her legs tight around me and fed a bite to me. We both chewed while she lowered her hand to direct me inside her. She squeezed her legs in a rhythm to pace our sex. In a moment she reached to the table for another bar to feed us as we sweated and pumped and abused our bodies like animals. It was great morning sex.

"Now ve svim, Anton," she said after.

"Sure," I said. I didn't dislike her at all, but I didn't know her well enough to like her very much. We had sex as much as we had conversation, which was easy since half the relationship required no thought. It was just biological.

I dated a few tennis players like her, a few models hoping to be actresses. The consistent threads between them were that they all had unconventional backgrounds and that I never got to know them much. It was a release and it was some company. It was a way to float, the way I was doing things on the court too.

An elite athlete must have a willingness to suffer. There's the endurance training through thresholds of physical pain. There's also the mental and emotional sacrifice to narrow the world. A willingness to suffer is either born in us or beaten in early. I believe mine was beaten in. Either way, I was losing my willingness.

CHAPTER

28

Another bad loss. My opponent had cracked a top-five world ranking but that was six years ago. He was ranked thirty-seven at the time of our match. He was twenty-nine years old so he had some tennis left in him, but still, I should be on my way up and he should be on his way out.

I was playing the Memphis Open. It was second round so the field hadn't narrowed down much. There were still lots of matches and a few guys coming and going in the locker room. I had my big tennis bag with extra rackets and my energy drink. I dropped it in front of my locker and sat down leaning forward with my forearms on my knees, thinking about the flight out of Memphis for the next tournament and how could I stop losing.

Jim Crane had beaten me. He skipped into the locker room behind me and dropped his bag but didn't sit. He jogged in place the way runners do when held at a stoplight. It was a ridiculous sight only twelve feet from me in a locker room that was otherwise sluggish and where eye contact was avoided.

Jim did a three-sixty still jogging in place. There were Jim, me and four other players in the room. "Hey, Christos," Jim said to a Spanish player on the tour. "Your match is tomorrow, right? Want to go hit some balls? There are a few things I want to work on."

No one looked up at Jim. Not even Christos. Everyone knew the message Jim was sending. Anton was no opponent today, he didn't push me, I ain't breathing heavy. What a dick. "Not today," said Christos.

"Alright, man. Anyone else? Otherwise I gotta go for a run. I gotta get someone to bring a pair of running shoes down here."

I wanted to break my racket over his face. I'd never seen such overt dick-ness. The match had actually gone three sets but he'd whooped me 6–1 in the third. I knew right when I was going to lose. It was early in the third set and I was facing break point when mentally I crossed over and predicted my own loss. I felt it coming. Once I knew that, I wanted it right away. Kill me quickly. He recognized it in me. So he killed me a little and I killed me a lot and it was over fast.

No one answered Jim so he said, "Alright." He took his phone from his bag. "I'm going to find some running shoes." He put the phone to his ear and jogged out.

I was too embarrassed to look up from my sneakers. Too embarrassed to unlace them, get undressed and get into the shower. Too embarrassed to move. Nobody spoke.

I wanted the room to clear. I stayed motionless, like Rodin's depressed and embarrassed *Thinker*. I wanted everyone gone before I moved, I wanted the whole exchange wiped away from memory, then I wanted to find Jim Crane and beat the crap out of him.

A hand rested on my shoulder. "You should take it as a compliment, Anton."

I was still bent forward and I looked up like a swimmer breathing to see Mark Woodbridge standing beside me. I'd never played Mark before, he was too old for that, but he was American and I knew him. He was a coach now and had been a doubles specialist and won some doubles Grand Slams. He was probably only late fifties but was weathered from too much sun and booze so that his skin was dry and lifeless like a brown leaf in winter.

He said, "Jim wouldn't bother doing that with a lesser player. All those theatrics."

"How do you mean?" I said.

"He's already thinking about the next match he'll have with you."

"By going for a jog?" I said.

"By getting in your head. He knows you have more talent, more firepower. The both of you playing great, straight up, you'll kill him. And you're younger. The only way he beats you is if he rattles you, breaks you down mentally. Like he did today."

I grunted.

"He was just getting started on it for next time. You'll probably see him again in the next month or two."

"He's a dick," I said.

"You're angry?"

"I'm pissed." I was extremely pissed.

"I'm happy to hear that," he said. "If it makes you feel any better, there are no true jerks in the world. There are only some unhappy people who behave like jerks," and he walked away.

That was a helpful moment for me. I had confused, misdirected rage and Mark helped me tap into it. I needed more rage. Good rage.

I had dealt with other losses. Plenty, and I had always managed to stomach them, move on. I told myself that part of tennis was that every couple weeks you took a loss. That's the way it is even for the top players.

But I'd never had a loss thrown in my face like this before. Humiliation during and after the fact, and it burned. Jim had set fire to a desperation I hadn't felt in a few years. I was always a competitor, always a champion, but that part of me had been crowded out. I had been distracted by all the things I had never had a chance to experience while under my father.

Now the part of me that needed to win was screaming out. Listen to me. Don't embarrass us again. Don't let a weaker player defeat and humiliate us, lord it over us like an enslaved enemy.

I still sat but my muscles were flexed and tight through my chest, arms and legs. I wanted to meet Gabe and Bobby, increase my practice and strength training, increase my testosterone and HGH intake. Obliterate Jim Crane on the court then go obliterate him off the court too.

CHAPTER

29

Jim Crane had beaten me in the early rounds so I had almost a week before my next trip. I used the extra time to go to my New York apartment that I had just rented, and scheduled a session with Dr. Minkoff.

I'd gotten very comfortable with Dr. Minkoff and I respected him. He was willing to share his thoughts with me. He wasn't so cautious a therapist that he only listened and gave prompts to keep me talking. The more he knew me, the more he revealed what his instincts were telling him about me.

I told him about the loss to Jim Crane and he said, "What you're learning is that you can't have it both ways."

I was in a deep leather chair and the leather was worn and soft so it felt like velvet.

Dr. Minkoff said, "You're talented, Anton. You're up against guys like Crane who are training around the clock and are so obsessed with winning that they're playing match mind games two months in advance. What you're thinking about is how you can have less training and more dates with girls. You're not that talented. Not so talented that you can keep this up and still beat guys like Crane."

"I guess not."

"So I suspect you're partly angry with Crane and partly angry with yourself. You can't be halfway into professional tennis and expect to win many matches. And the worst part of being halfway in is that you're dragged around by the half that is in. Physically dragged around the world for eleven months on the tour. It's not like you get half your life back. It's only the emotional half that's not in. Your actual life is still travelling with the tour, only you're going to lose to guys like Crane."

I could tell Minkoff loved me in a paternal way. He was angry for me, scared for me, wanted better for me. Of course everything he said made sense. I said, "I always thought my tennis career was meant to be, that I had this gift so my fate was to use the gift. Maybe that's been a mistake. Maybe it's all been a foolish errand."

He nodded. "You can stop playing. You can stop today." A reminder he'd offered before.

"Maybe Ana's a foolish errand too." Love or obsession, I still felt as strongly about Ana. All the other girls had been a way to get through to the time when Ana and I could be together. The girls were a sleeping pill to get to the next day.

"We've talked about fate. You're in control of all of this. Tomorrow morning you could be a retired player sitting in a plane on the way to see Ana."

"Sure."

"How would you feel tomorrow morning if that's what you were doing?"

I pictured it. Just an overnight bag, no rackets or tennis gear. Reading a book on the way to hold Ana. "Pretty happy." I also pictured a punter in a football jersey. "Also depends on how much she wants to see me. Anyway, I have unfinished business."

"Unfinished tennis business?"

"I couldn't go out like that."

"You were beaten and taunted by a lesser player."

"I'm pissed about that, of course that's part of it. But I've also never done anything close to what I'm capable of doing. I've never won a major. Whether I have loved or hated tennis, I've worked for that, sacrificed for that, taken steroids for that." I shook my head. "Maybe I need to increase my steroid program."

"Are you serious?"

"Why not? You're the one advising against being halfway in."

"Are you on a minimal program now?"

"I'm on only an oral program now. Testosterone and human growth pills. No needles, but I've talked to Bobby about it. We talked about it again after the Crane match."

"Are many players on the tour taking performance-enhancing drugs?"

"Doc, everyone. Everyone who's any good."

"Just players at the top?"

"It used to be just the top. Now it's the middle too, and anyone at the bottom who can afford it. They'd all like to get to the top one day too."

"I'm surprised. I knew baseball, some other sports. I didn't realize it was so prevalent in tennis."

"It's in every sport, doc," I said. "Golf too. Every sport has gone through a period of denial, the way tennis and golf are now. De-cades ago you would hear people say all the time, how can steroids help a man hit a baseball—you either hit it or you don't. Everyone's come to understand that steroids can help a man hit a baseball very much. Tennis is still at the beginning of the denial phase. Guys on the tour are the future Barry Bonds, Mark McGwire, Sammy Sosa of tennis. I'm one of those guys."

Listening to myself talk this way, I could hear that I had quietly become a veteran. Being the one to open another's eyes in this way was a rite of passage.

Dr. Minkoff shook his head. This news made the man who loved me like a son very sad. "Anton," he said after a moment. "What do you want to do?"

I said, "I want to increase my training program, in every way, focus on tennis, use all my firepower. Then I want to go out and obliterate people. I don't want to win, I want to put a beat-down on anyone I play."

Minkoff nodded. "Okay."

"I'll look up again at life a few years from now. First I'll finish this business."

We sat in silence together for a few full minutes. Finally he said, "Do you know of the economic theory of specialization?"

"Maybe I read about it."

"It was developed by David Ricardo. Comparative advantage. Imagine you're a tropical island and you can grow bananas like nobody's business. Bananas naturally grow well, but you'd have to work your ass off and use acres of land to turn out one potato. Of course you wouldn't bother with potatoes. You'd grow millions of bananas and trade some with Ireland when you want potatoes."

"Right."

"That's fine as a macroeconomic theory, fine for a country. Not

for a man. A man has to be a whole self. A man can't trade for character or life experience and he can't get those from a book either."

I shifted in the leather chair.

Dr. Minkoff said, "You are specialized, Anton. The danger for
an elite athlete like you is that you can get to be thirty years old
and all you've ever done is grow bananas." He held his stare with
me. He really wasn't cautious with me at all. "You were instructed
to grow bananas from the time you were six years old."

We were silent again, then I said, "You want me to quit tennis?"

"No. I want you to be prepared for when you do."

I knew what that meant more than I did even a few years ago.
"I'm working on that. I'm trying. Whether or not it's a mistake that
I ever started in on tennis, I'm in it now. It's not really who I am.
Not everything I am, anyway. It's all a masquerade but I'm so far
in that it can't end now. I don't want it to, and one thing I've realized is that the only way to succeed in tennis long-term is to stay
unconscious."

He said, "What do you mean by stay unconscious?"

He knew what I meant and he knew that the words were so
tragic that if I said them out loud they might give me pause so I
used his words instead. "Grow bananas."

It was late August. Ana was in New York City for meetings because she had written a play and was trying to get it produced on Broadway. Late August in the tennis schedule meant the US Open and New York City so we found ourselves in the same city at the same time and we went out to dinner.

I picked the Waverly Inn. We both would naturally prefer a place that is less of a scene but I wanted the night to be special so I picked a place where celebrities and paparazzi go, just in case the flashiness would give me support in making things special. I hired a car service for the night which was an investment of a few hundred dollars. Also, I could pick up Ana at her hotel so we could ride together rather than meet at the bar of the restaurant like people on a blind date.

Our driver pulled onto Bank Street and stopped in front of number 16 which had a speakeasy-style entrance and would be easy to pass by except for the two tabloid photographers on the sidewalk a respectful ten yards from the restaurant door. We had an 8:30pm reservation so there was only the gray light of dusk in summer.

I told the driver to stay put and I came around to get the door for Ana.

"Thank you, sir," she said as she took my hand and stepped up from the car.

"Ana," one of the photographers called.

I took her arm in mine and escorted her like we'd been introduced at a state dinner. I initiated the arm clasp though she was willing.

"Ana, look over here please." She looked to the right at the photographers who had cameras ready against their faces. Flashes popped. Ana smiled and waved.

"Thank you!" they said. A few more flashes. They were actually nice.

A moment later I heard one say to the other, "Is that Anton Stratis?" Then, "Anton! Anton, would you look this way?"

Nice. I smiled and waved, held Ana closer. Maybe they'd post the photos somewhere so her boyfriend would see them. Not a kind thought, but I couldn't help having it.

The entrance led to a small crowded bar with a low ceiling and little light. The hostess greeted us right away by name and took us around the side of the bar through a short corridor of booth-style seating to an open room of dining tables. A table was set for us in the corner. It gave us a bit of audio-privacy but was where the other tables could see us, which is how the restaurant liked it and how most celebrities liked it too.

I hustled around Ana and the hostess to the chair with its back to the corner and pulled it out for Ana. I was being my best gentleman self. I was in competition with some actor I'd never met.

"How'd your meetings go?" I said.

"Exciting." Once in a while you can see a person in real life who doesn't look real. Their body isn't bound by the same properties of light, doesn't seem bound by anything earthly. Anyone who walked in that room would see she wasn't like anyone else. She glowed the way a half dozen or so people in each generation do. Grace Kelly. Marilyn Monroe. "I met with a producer who can pull this off. Broadway is a whole other world of unions and insider stuff that I've never dealt with so I need someone strong."

"He's in?"

"It's early, but he wants to be. We sort of mapped out a plan. Do a short run off Broadway, then a six-month run on Broadway."

"And you'll star in it?"

"Writer, director, actor."

"I'm impressed."

"Writer and director are the ones I care about. Actor is the one everyone else cares about, so I get to write and direct only if I act too. That sells the tickets."

"You sound like you don't want to act," I said.

"The acting part is good. No one should complain about being in the movies or on stage, so I'm grateful but acting is about ten percent of what I want to do and right now the acting is going well enough that I can use it as a platform to break into these other areas. In thirty years, I won't be so in demand. There aren't many Meryl Streeps out there staying busy over the decades."

Our worlds were different but our problems were the same. Our culture made alluring careers of child games, then abruptly cut off the oxygen to those careers when we were barely more than kids.

She said, "I don't think I could be Meryl and I don't want to be. I want to be more like Amanda Peet."

"You're a much bigger star than Amanda Peet."

"She's a successful playwright. I love writing. In fifty years, I can still do what I love."

My face betrayed something. Envy, maybe. The pain of a direct hit. I said, "That's the dream." I was twenty-four. I could be out of tennis in a few years, ten at the extreme most. Fifty years more of life, in or out of tennis, was incomprehensible.

"How's tennis going?"

How deep to go into my response? She was safe, and wise too, but I wanted her to love me, not heal me. "I am reborn a tennis player."

"What does that mean?"

"I should just have Minkoff send you my file."

"You're seeing him still?"

"I am, he's great. Thank you."

She smiled.

I said, "It means I haven't been very focused on tennis the last few years but I'm going to commit myself now. I'd like to feel that I've done one thing great, and I do only one thing. So that's why I'm reborn. I haven't figured out what my version of writing and directing is."

We ordered salads, entrees and a bottle of wine. The waiter was attentive but didn't try to put on any kind of performance for us. These kinds of restaurants are very careful with celebrity clients.

When the waiter left, Ana said, "Have you thought about what you might do after tennis?"

"Every time I set my mind to that I draw such a blank that I terrify myself. It always ends with an image of me as a listless, pathetic loser at age thirty-five."

It occurred to me that this was not the way to woo her, but she laughed and said, "That would never be you. You're too smart. Thoughtful."

I tasted the wine, then asked the waiter to pour.

Ana said, "Coaching?"

"No, I don't think so. There are great players who retired, fed up with tennis and never imagined coaching and are back in the game coaching now, but I'd do that only as a last resort. If everything else were a dead end."

She said, "Are you happy?"

Good question. I hadn't put it to an up or down vote in a while, a simple summation. Probably because it's not so simple, nor is it the same day to day. "No." I paused, then said, "I'm not unhappy either, really. And I think I can be happy. If I get a few things right."

"An optimist."

"I'm out from underneath my dad. I'm myself now, so that's a good start." The salads came. Food and drink are good props to reset eye contact and posture naturally. I could have confessed my steroid use, how it was a sacrifice I hated but made with certainty. I think I held back from fear. Maybe she would see it as too dark and unforgivable. Instead I said, "Are you happy?"

She took her time finishing a bite of salad then said, "I am. Now."

"You were not when?"

"When my uncle was molesting me. When my mother knew and did nothing about it."

Wow. It was an abrupt and frank confession. She could let a guy know information like that is on the way. A small preamble. "I'm sorry."

"I'm better. It took a lot of time, effort, but I'm better." She sipped her wine. "Some people survive terrible experiences then say that even though it was terrible, they're glad they went through it, wouldn't trade it, because it made them who they are and they've gotten to like themselves. I can understand that but in my case I would trade it away in a second. I would trade away some of the goodness of who I am if I could trade away all the times he abused me. All the times my mother pretended."

We all have problems. Many people would say I was emotionally abused as a child, but there was a difference between bad and severe and I knew it. "Where is your uncle now?"

"Out of my life."

"Your mother?"

"It's cordial but empty. We talk on the phone about two times a year."

We were quiet for a long time. When the entrees came we talked about lighter things. Good movies to see. Hotels and museums in different cities that we liked. The kind of things we'd only ever done with other people but that I'd like to do with her. Had imagined doing with her many times.

Our conversation had easy transitions between heavy and light, dark and light, so I said, "We both have had trouble getting close to people, trusting people. I know I have anyway, and maybe you have. In our lives these walls have gone up and I think of them as external and internal walls. The external walls are social isolation. The internal walls are emotional isolation. You have some internal walls. The problem with professional tennis is that it causes both. It's ironic because most people think of tennis as one of the social sports. You play with some friends, tell jokes, afterward you drink beer and lemonade. That's tennis for most people but professional tennis is an external wall, so high you can't see over it." I was still on my first glass of wine and had barcly touched it but sipped it then. I thought about telling Ana about Liz but decided not to. Still humiliating after all those years. "You got over the external wall to me. The internal wall too." If that didn't say I love you, I didn't know what would.

I watched her. "Anton, that's . . ." She was blushing. "Really beautiful."

I said, "Have you ever read Lucretius?" I knew this was geeky but she wanted to be a writer and I thought it might work out okay.

"No."

"He was a Roman, he wrote *On the Nature of Things,* and he was a follower of Epicurus, a Greek philosopher. Some people think Epicureanism is about indulging and orgies and is anti-religion, but it's not. One of the main things is that the key to happiness is human relationships, here on earth."

The blushing was gone. She was over that and on to something else. "I believe that's true. When I think of my happiest moments, more and more of the recent ones involve other people and that wasn't the case ten years ago. I'm happier now than I was then."

Who were those other people she was having happy moments with? Ryan Hall. Damn. "That's good to hear," I said. "Ryan must be a nice guy." I said it. I couldn't help but bring it up. They'd been dating off and on for years and I had read recently that it was back on.

"He's a good guy."

Measured praise? It seemed that way. I hoped. "I'm sure."

She said, "We've had some happy moments, though I have to say we've never had a conversation like this one."

This sounded very good. "What does he like to talk about?"

"Topics might include changes to his gym routine suggested by his personal trainer, new research on nutrition, players the Clippers are evaluating in the upcoming NBA draft."

"All interesting." Now we were making fun of Ryan. This was deadly stuff.

"That's not really fair of me." She laughed. "He's smart and interesting. He reads a lot. Maybe not Lucretius, but screenplays, some novels."

"Of course." I needed to be gentle with Ryan here. Stay above it. I was pretty sure the damage was already done anyway. Ryan was toast.

"He wants to go from teenage heartthrob actor to serious actor. He might be able to do it."

I felt a little sorry for Ryan then. He probably had many of the same issues Ana and I did. "I'm sure he'll figure something out."

That night I kissed Ana goodnight on her cheek by the elevator in her hotel lobby. I was sure we both wanted more but this was the way to end our night. We had built something strong between us. A human connection of knowledge and trust. It's possible to come to know a person so that you know just how they'll be when they're with you and there's a happy anticipation of seeing them the way there is for a return trip or repeat holiday.

Days later the US Open started and I was winning with such authority that the media started talking about me as the favorite to win the tournament. I was unbeatable up to the finals when my leg cramped in the second set, then I had to retire the match in the third set.

I would like to say my success on the courts was due entirely to my success at the Waverley Inn but there was another new influence on my tennis in those weeks. Bobby was giving me what he called candy poppers. Small hits of testosterone in a jellybean.

He calculated my weight and metabolism to measure precisely

enough for a four-hour hit. If a match ended quickly and I got tested, I needed to hold my pee and watch the clock.

It was risky but it was worth it. Everyone should get to try it once. There was a large boost in energy but more surprising was the boost in focus, even determination. My vision seemed to go from twenty/twenty to twenty/ten. I could hear everything cleaner, make distinctions between all the different tiny sounds, process the information and react. I was a weapon.

Ben Archer had made it to the semis on the other side so I didn't face him but he put in another good tournament. Steady Ben. Easy Ben. Content Ben, growing bananas. How the hell did he do it?

31

I would set all meetings with Bobby and Gabe by then. I made it clear that I didn't want our discussions shared with Dad. I didn't want him to be involved in any way. There can be no influence if there's no knowledge.

Dad had gotten resentful that he was out, off the team. He'd joke with me that I had fired him and he'd say he wondered where was his severance package. He'd taken up trying to coach local kids at the high school and the club, looking for another pro prospect.

But I needed Dad out. The Anton Stratis enterprise would rise or fall with me in charge. I took this role on and not without anxiety, but I had to take it. I couldn't be a champion on the court and someone's lieutenant off it.

The US Open was the last major of the season. The majors wouldn't start again until the Australian in January, so I went into the rest of the hard court season at twenty-five years old never having won a major.

I said to Bobby, "It's working. My body is still adjusting but the candy poppers definitely work."

"How do you feel?"

Gabe never joined the meeting when we talked about drugs. Of course he knew and he probably rounded back with Bobby later to make sure he was fully in the loop with my training. He just didn't want to be in the meeting. Whatever made people feel a little better about things was fine with me. I said, "I need to get stronger."

"We're through the busiest part of the season. If you skip the November tournament, we can get almost eight straight weeks off to devote to training. We'll adjust the conditioning program, focus on building up some muscle."

I nodded. "Stronger than that."

"Okay." He trailed the word into a question mark.

"I want to accelerate the whole program. Everything," I said. Bobby had been pushing a broader drug program for a while and I had been resisting up to now.

"Alright. I can lay out some options for you."

"I know the option I want."

Bobby wasn't certain what I meant. His face said clue me in.

"I'm not doing anything half-assed now." I pointed at his chest. "You do whatever it takes." There, I said it. Whatever it takes.

It was a moment between us, something to build on and remember when the work got hard, an exchange of words to print up on T-shirts. I could hear the Rocky training music start playing in my head and I watched Bobby, wondering if he'd say, "What are we waitin' fer," like Burgess Meredith.

Instead, he said, "There's a mix I've been looking at that's having some success out there. It's three elements but we'd do it in a single shot, oil-based so we need a wide gauge needle. I'll dose it out so we need one hit per week. Side of the upper butt and we'll alternate sides so there should be no issues."

Right to business. He had been ready for this. "And the tests?"

"Everything in the mix will be under the radar."

"This mix gets results?"

"You'll be a beast." He smiled. He liked doing his job well.

I didn't feel sad at all. I'd become numb to considerations of morality in sport. I wanted advantage. "Good," I said. "Let's dial it up."

I had a mental slip then and returned to the what-if question I'd had before. What if I was never meant for tennis, this was all a mistake, a lie, but here I was worshipping at the altar of my false tennis gods, sacrificing, self-flagellating.

Then I regained balance from my mental slip, beat the questions away. I told myself this was time-limited and I could do anything if it was time-limited. My usual logic. "I need to see Gabe now. Thanks, Bobby."

I slid off the training table in the back room of the Florida gym where Bobby and I met for strength training. I drove to the tennis club where I had a practice session scheduled with Gabe.

He was standing midcourt, leaning on the net post when I swung open the wire door. "Ready to work?" he said.

"I am."

He straightened up and twirled his racket. I said, "I just had a good meeting with Bobby."

"Oh?"

I put a hand on Gabe's shoulder. He was so much shorter than me. He was shorter even when we first met but I wasn't a boy anymore. Our relationship had changed. He had gone from a sort of camp counselor to a professional colleague, and I was the boss. He provided a service for which I paid. I said, "This is our year, Gabe. It happens now."

He knew exactly what Bobby and I had met about.

32

Making the finals of the US Open raised my profile. I followed up the Open by winning the next two hard court tournaments so I was back in the conversation of top players to watch. My world ranking was eleven and moving in the right direction.

My agent signed two endorsement deals, one for razor blades and one for an energy drink. Good money, and the camera crews flew to me to make quick and easy TV spots. There are step-change moments in fame that a person can feel happening. More double-takes and whispers happen on the periphery, an entire ecosystem shift, like moving as a guest from a Holiday Inn to the presidential suite of the Four Seasons where everyone had memorized my name and said it with a slight bow.

I went to parties, the same kind of parties I'd gone to for years, but people decided I was a different person. I used to hug a drink to my chest and pull out my phone to pretend there were emails that needed attention so that I wouldn't appear to be a friendless mute. Now I couldn't handle the incoming, couldn't find time to break away for another drink. My face had been on enough American TVs during the Open that people recognized me and wanted to congratulate me. There'd be five or six people waiting in semicircle formation for their turn, and there were famous people. Actors, musicians, politicians, and they wanted to talk to me, treated me as though I were the celebrity, not the other way around. It gave me a sense of not belonging. Someone else belonged here and if I ever became that someone else, how much connection would there be to the old me?

Andre Agassi invited me to play in a pro-am in Los Angeles to benefit his foundation. I'd have said yes anyway because I liked what I knew of Agassi and wanted to meet him. He'd also asked Ana to be one of the celebrity amateurs. There was a strong current going my way.

We played the event on the courts of the UCLA campus where Agassi sold tickets to watch and auctioned off lunches with his celebrity friends. Some calls from my agent secured Ana as my mixed doubles partner and we played against Steffi Graf and some guy from *Dancing With the Stars*.

Ana got to the court after me, wearing a pleated white tennis miniskirt and a white jog bra, and she started stretching by the net. I stood like a kid on the beach of Cape Canaveral watching a shuttle launch. I'd have been caught staring except no one was looking at me. We were all watching the same thing, even the women.

You can know the whole of a woman's body from seeing her calves and shoulders. If those are great, everything between is great too. Ana had perfect lines of feminine muscle along her thighs and hamstrings to a skinny knee then a rounded calf muscle and slim ankle.

"Hey partner," she said.

"Of all the gin joints, etc., etc.," I said.

She laughed. "Don't give me that. Your agent's request was passed on to me for approval. Or disapproval."

"Glad you approve."

"Well, I plan on winning this thing. Steffi's past her prime."

Ana played very well for a social player. She had the natural form people get only if they've had lots of lessons at a young age. It gave me hope that she'd been concealing what a fan of tennis she was.

Steffi was composed and kind and as the gracious hostess, she let us win the match, despite Ana deliberately hitting her serve into my back three times. Really the paying ticket holders wanted to see Ana leap up and down in victory and at an event like this you've got to give the people what they want.

We had two hours before a cocktail reception that Andre was hosting and after that day I had no idea when I'd see Ana next. The four of us in the match took photos at the net then I said to Ana, "Come with me."

Ana had an assistant and a security guard who met her at the side of the court but I took her hand and said, "We have urgent business."

"I'll see you later," she told them, and I led her off in a jog so people couldn't stop us for autographs. Agassi had converted the lobby of an administrative building near the courts into a player lounge away from the crowds. It was a five-story building of offices and I had hopeful and perverted thoughts of what might happen tucked away in one of them.

"Where are we going?"

Years of playing it cool up in smoke, an explosion of a pent-up, childish crush. "Somewhere quiet to talk."

We came through the lounge still hand in hand and jogging because I couldn't stand the idea of anyone stopping us. There were some hellos that I brushed away with a wave and kept running like a halfback at half speed, ready to accelerate to the opening when it appeared.

There were double doors at the end of the room with the kind of latch that released by pressing on the horizontal bar. I rammed through and we slowed to a walk on the stairs.

"Are you okay?" Ana said.

"Yeah," I said. "I'm great." We were still holding hands. "You played really well. I had no idea."

"Don't patronize me."

"I'm serious. You looked great."

She smiled. "Why are we running around an office building?"

We were on the landing, halfway between the first and second floors. I pulled her hand and brought her into me like a waltz partner and my other arm went around her lower back. She pressed her hips and stomach against mine. Different answers sprinted through my head. *Because I need to kiss you. Because I need to hold you. Because I need to tell you that I love you.* I brought my hands up so that my palms went along her cheeks and jawline, barely touching, just enough for the tender act of contact the way an archeologist would lift the Holy Grail, and I kissed her. First soft, then harder, then harder still as she kissed back and brought her arms around my shoulders.

I tasted the salt of her drying sweat and lowered a hand down her back to her tennis skirt and pulled her in tighter.

"This was a long time coming," she said.

"Yes."

She affirmed the moment by kissing my cheek then neck and held my shoulders.

The door just below us swung open and banged into the wall. It was Adam.

"Hey," he said, staring, unmoving, embarrassed but not embarrassed enough to retreat. "They," he paused, "said you came through this way."

"Correct," I said, pissed off that he hadn't left yet.

"I need to have a word." He held up his phone. "It's Gabe and Bobby." Adam had travelled with me to the pro-am. Gabe and Bobby were back in Florida. I'd never before had a conference call with the two of them.

"Ana, I'll be right back." I realized how absurd it would be for her to wait in the cement stairwell. "I'll see you in the lounge. This should be only a few minutes."

I walked down and took the phone from Adam. "I'm here."

"Are you someplace you can talk privately?" said Gabe.

His tone pushed aside my annoyance over the interruption. "One minute." I walked through the lounge to the lawn outside. "Okay. Shoot."

"You haven't heard about Jian Liang yet?"

"No, what are you talking about?"

"He's dead," said Gabe. "It's all over the web."

I hadn't played Jian Liang in almost a year. He was the top-ranked player from China and ranked number seven in the world. He was about my age. "How?"

"There are about ten different stories going around and pretty much all of them involve steroids," said Gabe.

Bobby's voice came on the line. "There's a story that it was a bad transfusion. Another that he was trying a new cocktail of things and it was a bad combination. Stopped his heart. Another that his injection went directly into an artery, killed him."

"That doesn't matter right now," Gabe cut him off. "Right now the media's going to be all over this and you need to keep low until you decide how to handle it."

I looked over to the courts fifty yards away where ten reporters and cameramen were moving like bees from stigma to stigma. A reporter glanced up and we made eye contact. He with a micro-phone in someone's face, I with a phone pressed to my head, and we watched each other for a moment. Others looked over at me.

I was a strange sight, standing alone on a large green lawn in bright white tennis clothes. A field mouse beneath circling hawks. "I need to get inside."

I walked back to the lounge and waved to Ana who was talk-ing with Adam and three others who had come to admire her. I went back to the stairwell landing.

"Okay, I'm good," I said. "Look, I think this is pretty simple. It's a tragic death, steroids are bad, I don't do them."

"They're going to press you," said Gabe. "They won't let it be simple."

"I can handle it."

"Okay, Anton. Answer this. Does tennis have a steroid prob-lem?"

"I don't think so."

"That's not a no. So it might have a steroid problem?"

"No, no. It doesn't."

"Jian Liang is dead, allegedly from steroids. Have you ever heard of any other steroid use on the tour?"

"Of course there have been some positive tests and penalties, and you hear rumors."

"What rumors?"

I was getting Gabe's point. "Just silly stuff." I was squirming as though Gabe was a real reporter.

"Where did you hear the rumors? Who told you?"

"I'd rather not say."

"You're blown away," said Gabe. "A reporter just blew you out of the water."

I made a long exhale trying to let out the stress. "Shit," I said.

"Let's run through this. Say that you don't know the details but you'd be shocked if steroids were involved. Liang was a great player. There have been small incidents of cheating in the past on the tour but the ATP has dealt with that. Tennis is a clean sport and to your knowledge there are zero players cheating today."

"Right," I said. The news started to trickle into me and get personal. Poor Liang. I didn't know him really. He wasn't Chinese-American, he was Chinese-Chinese so nobody on the tour really knew him. I bet we had a lot in common. We were both top tennis players and there weren't many different ways to do that.

"Bobby, not for nothing, in case this was a bad combination of drugs, let's triple check what I'm putting in my body."

33

One month later I got an invitation to celebrate terrible news.

ANA STOKKE AND CALEB CASA

INVITE YOU TO CELEBRATE THE ANNOUNCEMENT OF

THEIR ENGAGEMENT

PLAZA HOTEL, NEW YORK CITY

7:30PM

Caleb Casa was the first thirty-million-dollar man. More than Jennifer Lawrence, George Clooney, Tom Cruise. I read that if you added the percentage he got on the back end, he made almost $80 million on his last picture.

The invitation arrived one day prior to the phone call that was meant to soften the blow.

"Anton."

"Hi." I tried to sound aloof.

"How are you?"

"Great."

"Are you in Florida?"

"I got your invitation. Thanks."

Long pause. "I'm sorry. I wanted to speak with you first. I wasn't even sure if I should invite you but I consider you a friend. A dear friend, and of course you would find out about it anyway. Probably naïve, but I'm hoping you'll be happy, hoping you'll come if you can."

"I'm sure that's what a dear friend would do."

She said nothing.

"Things were pretty different thirty days ago. In Los Angeles."

"I know. I should explain." She took a beat. "Caleb and I had been seeing each other. The press hadn't picked it up and we weren't all that serious but we'd been talking about getting more serious. When I got back from Los Angeles I started to tell him about you. Caleb asked if we could take a vacation together to talk it out and it worked for our schedules so we went to Hawaii. It just went really well. We connected, I guess." She paused again. "On the last day there he proposed."

"Congratulations." This struck my most raw nerves.

"I'm sorry."

"I feel deceived." I was proud of that statement. It was the truth. I could have said something nasty or I could have pretended it didn't bother me. Instead I told her how I felt.

"I didn't mean to deceive you. What you did in L.A. was sudden, I never expected that."

"You knew I liked you, knew I had pushed for us to be doubles partners in the event."

"Doubles partners, fine, we're friends. I didn't know you were going to pull me into a stairwell and kiss me."

"Caleb never came up in conversation when I did."

"We were interrupted by your phone call and you left in the middle of the kiss!"

I was accusing her and that wasn't productive or fair. "Alright."

There was a long minute of silence. I didn't want to hang up. That felt like letting go of a helium balloon in the park, having to watch it rise away to a speck in the sky. There was going to be no good ending to the call.

She said, "I didn't want you to hear about it in tabloids. I didn't want you to learn about it from the invitation either. I'm sorry. You deserve much better than that."

After another long minute I said, "If I'm near New York then, I'll try to make it." We hung up.

My masochistic streak won again. Once I had rearranged my schedule and flown to New York, it was very convenient to be there for the party. I got to the Plaza at 8:15pm. If the room was already crowded I could pick my spots and hide if I needed to.

I took an elevator to an upstairs ballroom. I wore a tailored, charcoal suit, white shirt, no tie, hair combed. It was how I looked when filming Rolex commercials. My stomach was churning, literally making loud noises in the elevator, which never happened, even before matches.

When the elevator doors opened there was a greeter. She was prepared, knew the names and faces of the guests and she said, "Mr. Stratis, welcome. The party is right this way." She led me through double doors to a ballroom that was half filled by about a hundred people.

"Thanks." I looked for a bar. I didn't need a drink. I needed something to do with my hands.

The guest-to-bartender ratio was four to one. I asked for a beer and waited while a man in white jacket and black tie poured from a bottle into a tulip glass.

A man in his thirties to my left was regaling four others about the process of writing screenplays. He began four consecutive sentences with the words "You see, you have to. . . ." He seemed to know all there was to know. The others nodded to him, cornered in an open room.

"Anton." Not shouted across the room. It was soft, right behind me, then a hand on my shoulder.

"Hi."

"Thank you for coming." Simple, said only one time, didn't overdo it, and I knew she meant it.

I didn't say of course. That wouldn't have been true. "You look great." True.

She gave me a hug. It was too much too soon. I only half hugged back. It was awkward and I'm sure looked awkward to anyone watching, and it stifled our conversation. She said, "Will you meet Caleb?"

"What the hell," I said, then tried and failed to smile.

He had been close but a respectful few paces away with an eye on us.

"Anton, this is Caleb. Caleb, this is Anton." Her voice was nervous. I took some pleasure in that. Small consolation, but something.

"How ya doing, Anton!" Either delighted to see me, or gloating.

"Fun party."

"Glad you could come." He was more than a head shorter than me, impossibly great hair and sparse, quarter-inch whiskers that made up a goatee and dirty face that was just less than a beard. Handsome movie star.

Ana was pulled from us at the worst time. Some woman tugged her elbow to introduce her to some other woman. I knew he and I both felt it because we both looked after her as though she was still one of us and hoped she'd be back to say something in time to save the situation.

Enough time passed that it was absurd to keep staring at her back. We looked at each other. Caleb smiled and said, "Really. Good of you to come."

Translation: you're magnanimous in defeat. "I really came to ask you how you get your hair to look so good. You blow-dry?"

"I can read people," he said. "I know you have a romantic side."

"What else do you know?"

He smiled. "I just hope your romantic side will help you see your way forward to being happy for us."

Rubbing my face in it. "I'll work on that."

He nodded, glanced at Ana in another conversation. "I've been with a lot of beautiful women. The best." Obnoxious. He kissed the tips of his fingers then spread them in the air. "Ana's really something though." Obnoxious and disrespectful.

I was losing my cool. I put a hand on the top of his shoulder and looked down at him. "You're not good enough for her."

In a room without a hundred people and security I think he'd have been scared but he acted brave here. "Maybe not. But you know the great thing?"

"What's that?"

"I get the chance to find out." He put his hand up to shake as a way to make us step back from each other and end the conversation. When you shake hands and connect at the base of each other's thumb with palm over palm, you have a firm handshake. If you grab the guy farther down the hand, just over the fingers, you can crunch the hell out of his knuckles. Caleb's hands were small to start with and I wrapped his fingers exactly there. I've been swinging a tennis racket for twenty years so my right forearm is about twice the size of my left. I had an easy smile while I watched his eyes bulge and he otherwise took the pain without reaction.

"What are you two boys talking about?"

I let him go. "Just getting to know each other a bit." It was immature, but it was all I could do.

"Nice," she said though it was obvious to her that it was anything but.

"Anton was just saying how many beautiful women are on the tennis tour. He seems to be quite the lady's man."

I looked from him to Ana. "Congratulations on marrying a real prick."

Ana couldn't get a word out, then, "What?"

"Bye."

I walked to the double doors and didn't look back at anyone. The damn elevator held me up.

"Anton."

I was six inches in front of the closed elevator doors. I turned to her.

"What was that?"

"You must know. You must know him well enough by now to know exactly what that was."

"What I saw was you insulting me and my fiancé at our engagement party. Which isn't like you."

"You missed a few gems prior to that and anyway I call 'em as I see 'em. That guy doesn't care about you. Go ask Minkoff the definition of malignant narcissist and tell me it doesn't line up. He thinks he deserves you and any other girl he wants at the same time because he puts himself first."

She was listening close. There had to be a voice in her head saying the same thing.

I went on. "I may not have my shit together. Entirely together," giving myself a little credit, "but I would never treat you that way. Never even think of you that way."

She nodded. Did I get through? Did she see the light? "I shouldn't have invited you." Oh well.

Caleb stuck his head out the double doors. "Let that jerk go."

The elevator doors opened, and she did.

Moving up the thirty spots in rank from fifty to twenty is much easier than moving the ten spots from twenty to ten, and every spot up from ten is hard as hell.

After a great finish to the year before, I'd started this year the same way. I won the Australian Open. My first major. Of the four, it's the one that I and the rest of the world care the least about, but it got that monkey off my back. I lost in the finals of the French Open even though clay was not a naturally good surface for my game and I didn't have it figured out then. I'd entered four other tournaments and won all four.

Grass court season started next and I entered the Queen's Club Championships in London, a grass court warm-up event to Wimbledon. I hadn't dropped a set on the way to the finals. I was healthy, strong, focused. I sat in the locker room before the finals match drinking Bobby's energy drink, watching the clock to time the candy popper exactly.

Gabe walked back in. "I just confirmed it with the ATP. If you win today, when they publish the points tomorrow, you'll be the new number one player. Number one. In the world."

I sipped my drink and nodded. "Well, I better win."

Gabe smiled. "No pressure."

I looked at the clock on the wall. Took the popper. Number one in the world. It was what I wanted. I wanted to add some more wins at majors to that but I wasn't worried about them coming. They would. I was playing with confidence. Beating the best players. There was nobody whose game I feared. "Showtime," I said.

Ben Archer. He was quietly having a good year. He'd cracked the top ten but top five was tennis royalty and he wasn't there yet. He showed no frustration about that. He was sure of himself, ever-present, plodding along, always dangerous. I'd never known competitive tennis without Ben in the game. He was always there, a constant companion, doing it a little different, like a reflection of me on a warped surface.

"Good luck today, Anton," said Ben.

"I wish you'd be an asshole for once."

"Break a leg," he said.

It didn't matter that Gabe had told me I could take over the number one ranking with a win. He only confirmed with the ATP what everyone around the tournament had been saying for a week. Gabe just took the speculation out of it, which I suppose was a good thing, but I started the match tight.

I knew Ben's game, knew my game was better, if I played well. He always played the goddamn same. Steady and good. His mental toughness was unnerving, especially when I was already nervous.

My first serve percentage was low, I sprayed my forehand around though I wasn't even going for much and I knew that was part of the problem. I couldn't bring myself to swing out.

When a player is tight, it's the same involuntary response that brings blood to the vital organs when a person is cold. Muscles constrict, bringing everything closer to the core. There can be no fluid, full extension. I dropped the first set 6–3.

The saving grace was that the set ended on an odd number of games so I had a changeover to collect myself. The match was best of three sets. If I didn't turn my play around, someone else would be number one.

I burned some energy trying to hype myself up. I was nursing no injuries. It had been an easy week of matches so I wasn't battling fatigue. I remembered how early in Rafa's career he would jump around at net in front of his opponent before a match then sprint from the net to the baseline. It was weird behavior and it threw people, like a fighter who stands in his corner between rounds instead of taking his chair.

At the end of the changeover I did a run with high knees to my baseline then did a set of short sprints along the baseline from side to side of the court. I never looked at Ben but knew he was watching and wondering what the hell I was doing.

The second set started on my serve and I knew if I could come out serving big it would feel to everyone that I had cast a spell, performed a freak incantation on the court. Turn the match around, magically.

The running around actually did loosen my muscles up. It also amused and distracted me. My best serve for an ace was power up the middle. I blasted two in a row to go up 30–love.

Ben smiled. It wasn't a genuinely amused smile. It was a that-son-of-a-bitch smile.

The next two serves I sliced wide, both aces. Four swings and a love service game to me. I took the second set 6–2.

Steady Ben knew I wasn't a magical creature and knew he was still in the match. He kept coming right at me, playing strong and smart. In the third and final set we were tied at 4 games each on Ben's serve.

So much of winning a match is the result of the decisions before the ball is in play. Which way was he going with the serve. Especially with the power serves in the game, it helps to decide, play the odds like at a craps table. Players don't guess on every serve but they do guess a lot and tournaments are won or lost depending on whether a guy bets the pass line.

These points are less about the shot-making. At our level we all made the shots most of the time.

I knew Ben's game so well. He was a strong enough player that for him to play to his strength was not a stupid plan. He didn't need to try to surprise people. At 4 all, deuce, in the deciding set, he'd play to his strength, and to the deuce court he liked to spin his serve out wide to take me off the court.

His toss went up and I slid a step over to the right. He started the whip of his racket up to the ball and I skipped twice farther to the right and began the rotation of my shoulders to be ready for a forehand. The serve came wide, right to where I was already waiting for it.

I caught the ball on the rise out of my service box and ripped a straight forehand up the line. Ben never moved for it. He turned to the ball boy behind him, got another ball and prepared to serve again. My ad.

He served into my body and I fought it off with a backhand return that floated high and deep to his backhand corner. Off the racket I knew it would drop in and with some cheap topspin so I closed into net behind it. Ben never saw me come in. He hit a backhand cross that was meant to be a deep, safe shot but it floated to the net high and soft like popcorn. I hit a smash that bounced up into the stands.

I had an easy hold of my serve to win the match. Tomorrow morning the world would wake up to a new number one tennis player.

PART III

Achievement marks the end of endeavor and the
beginning of despair.

—AMBROSE BIERCE

35

M y older brother was getting married. The reception was in the ballroom of the Philadelphia Country Club, about ten minutes from where I grew up. There's one week between the end of Queen's Club and the start of Wimbledon so I made the flight home.

Panos was marrying a girl who had gone to school nearby at Baldwin but they didn't really know each other until they were introduced in college and started dating. They'd been living together about six years, since graduation, so the wedding felt like a recognition of a commitment they'd already made.

I was best man for Panos. He and Kristie had to schedule the wedding for middle of the week in June so it wouldn't interfere with my play on the tour. The first decision about the wedding was about me, and that dynamic continued. I didn't spend much time with Dad in those days and he was thrilled to have an event to show off the world's new number one tennis player to his friends and he would tell them that he had foreseen my current ranking at the time of my birth. He was an insufferable partner in wedding planning for Panos and Kristie. He wanted to make sure they didn't hog the spotlight from me.

Panos took it with the same mix of relief and sadness he always did. It hurts not to be chosen by your own father, but to be chosen is worse. Panos preferred to be orphaned, which was a strong motivator to marry and have a life with Kristie. He wanted to start a family because ours wasn't much of one for him. His relationship with our father had become more like nephew to uncle.

"A toast!" yelled Dad, drunk, smacking his water glass with a spoon like he always did.

Lots of clapping in anticipation of his words, mostly from older people Dad's age, all his friends he'd crammed onto the guest list at the last moment. He was paying the tab for the party. Poor Kristie.

Dad raised a hand like calling for a pass and the clapping died out. Panos sat at a table for two with Kristie at the head of the room. I was next to him at a table for ten, stuffed with Dad's friends, Dad and Mom. There were four hundred guests in all. He said, "I couldn't be more proud of my boys!" He looked at Panos first, thank God, then over at me. "This has turned into a real celebrity wedding."

The words made me think of Ana who I wished could have been with me. I told her only that there was a wedding, hoping she'd invite herself which was absurd because nobody invites themselves to weddings, and of course she didn't. She had her own to plan.

Dad went on, "As we welcome this wonderful woman to our family," he gestured at Kristie, "we also welcome the number one tennis player in the world to our family," and he gestured at me. He was humiliating himself. Could anyone not find him appalling?

Kristie clapped, along with about half the people there. Class act. Panos had a smile etched in stone. He'd lived this too long to be surprised. I supposed he thought he might have had this day to himself, and he really might have if I hadn't just taken over number one. Bad luck.

"Panos and Anton grew up thick as thieves. Of course Anton was always the better player and while I was always pushing Anton on the tennis court, by the way, you're welcome, tennis fans, Panos was always pushing Anton to the movie theater or to some goof-off." He belly-laughed as though this had been a resounding punch line delivered spectacularly.

"The truth is," he went on, "Panos played an important role then. I could be very hard on Anton. You have to be hard if you want greatness. You have to break things down then build them back up, and Panos was always there to help build Anton back up. Through all the years of hard work, sweat, frustration, anxiety that it all may not work out, through all that chaos, Panos was a trusted friend, confidant, ally. Exactly what it means to be a brother."

These were all nice sentiments to express, maybe if I were inducted into the Tennis Hall of Fame. Even though he kept trying to round it back to Panos, thinking he was doing good, the entire context was wrong. I looked at Mom who wouldn't look at me.

"And so I say to you, Kristie, that not only do you have a good and loving husband in Panos, but you have, and I speak for our family, all of us."

She should decline the offer. She toasted though, then walked over to Dad and hugged him. He gave her a long embrace, certain he'd done something to be proud of.

I stood without attacking my water glass. Others around me started clinking and eyes turned to me for the best man toast.

"My favorite memories in my life all involve Panos." Kissing Ana and getting the number one ranking are up there, the rest are all with Panos. "Growing up I was OCD. I don't mean that as a euphemism for uptight. I had a strong case of the real thing." I looked at Panos. "I would marvel at my older brother. How did he make living look so easy? How did he make fun come so naturally? If I could draw up a perfect day, it would be to walk to the creek by our old house with our old fishing rods and spend the afternoon sitting on the bank of the creek fishing with Panos. Or going out to the movies with Panos. Or getting a ride with Panos to McDonald's for lunch. Anything for more time with my older brother." I looked at him. He had a smaller, relaxed smile. A real smile.

I said, "I still marvel at his charmed way of being." I didn't know Kristie well. Just small amounts of time here and there because I'd been on the road as long as they'd been together. I knew enough to like her and to know that they loved each other. "He meets and falls in love with a woman who has the same magnetism, the same way of lifting up everyone around them just by being there." I raised my champagne glass. "To the bride and groom."

Kristie came over and hugged me, followed by Panos. While he and I hugged, Dad appeared and hugged us both at once. He meant well, I was pretty sure.

Dad said to us, "Hey, I started working with this young kid at the club. Twelve years old and I'm telling you, he could be another you, Anton. Maybe better. Shows promise to be even better. Maybe not as athletic, but the mental toughness. Man."

This was quite a backhand to my own mental toughness. Typical from him. "Not now, Dad."

"Well, sure, of course. You fired me."

"Not now, Dad," I said again.

"Fine, you're right." He walked away. He was always worse with a few drinks.

The dinner part of the reception began to break up and people moved to the bar and dance floor. I found Panos and said, "I'm sorry about Dad."

"Don't be. We've always both been a little jealous of what the other has had." He clapped my shoulder and said, "You're handling him well."

"So are you."

"It's not so hard," said Panos. "I probably won't spend much time with him again until we have a kid. Then not again until the next kid."

I laughed. I hoped Kristie was having fun. Panos wanted to run away from his own wedding. A few of his groomsmen hustled over and circled us.

"Anton, let me shake your hand," one of them said and we did. "The hand that held the rackets that played the best tennis in the world has touched my hand." He held his own hand up and rotated it for inspection like it was now gold-leafed.

Most of Panos's good friends were from his college tennis team so they were all very into the game. They were drunk and playing around but still nervous around me, like I was otherworldly.

Becoming number one had created that effect on people, especially because I spent my life in close proximity to the tennis tour and was surrounded by people connected to tennis. I had become a known name in the world at large but I didn't live in the world at large. I lived in the tennis world where I was a god. Not the current-day Christian God who needs to be interpreted and defended. I was Zeus to ancient Greece, whose bizarre and humanlike qualities caused awe and fear. The more bizarre my demand, the more panic there was to see it done.

My life on the tour and people's reactions to me had changed. Whatever transportation, clothing, accommodation, meal, beverage I wanted, someone would get it for me. If I wanted five thousand green M&M's, and only green, someone would sort them out. A thousand pigs slaughtered in my honor, no one would question the justness.

I didn't even have to deal with people other than my own people most times. My agents, my coach or Adam, who'd become more of an assistant than racket stringer. There were handlers at each event who would ask my team how I wanted things, then they'd take care of it. I showed up, played and was otherwise pampered.

My stardom created more attention and so I had more insulation to intercept the attention.

Panos's friends wanted some war stories from the tour which I gave while he escaped to dance with Kristie, then I escaped to the bar.

Wedding guests rotated to me at the bar like an alternate receiving line so there was never an empty moment. Most got in and got out with only a handshake or word of congratulations. Some had a story they felt would compel my interest but through the numbing constancy of it I was half listening and offering meaningless responses. Normally, handlers would usher me through a crowd like this and I would never be so exposed.

I had managed two drinks when a striking blonde, my height with her heels on, approached with no intention of getting in and back out, nor did she offer congratulations or a handshake. She said,

"You'll never get out of this corner if I don't get you to the dance floor."

She was a friend of Panos from college. She'd played on the women's tennis team and had gone on to a modeling career, living in New York City. My fear of dancing had waned over the years and it sounded better than shaking hands. "Lead on."

She did, taking my hand and pulling me through a dozen bystanders like an airlift rescue. She had the strong, lean hands of a six-foot female athlete. She weaved to the center of the dance floor then turned to me and found the rhythm of the music while sliding up and down against my body. She'd had more to drink than I had.

Others on the dance floor gave us a few yards of space and watched. My dance partner was extremely good looking and well versed in attention.

With the next song we moved on to some bastardization of the Charleston, the two of us holding hands while we stepped away and back toward each other, then a series of twirls and spins performed by her. I knew a few of the building blocks of that kind of dance so we just repeated them with lots of energy, both of us performing.

She flung herself into a twirl and while my hand held her upraised hand over her head, her heel streaked over a wet spot on the floor. Her leg was uselessly airborne and as her body fell, her strong hands clenched my ring finger and pinkie only, the weakest two fingers of my playing hand.

Her ass fell in such a direct line to the floor that she bounced, still holding my now sprained fingers days before Wimbledon. Through pain and panic of injury, I helped her up and asked if she was okay.

She was as embarrassed as I was panicked, but otherwise fine so we retreated to the bar with less panache than the way we'd left it.

My evening ended an hour later with ice on my hand and me wondering how I'd manage to get by without my handlers.

36

The following morning I met Panos and Kristie for brunch at the restaurant they had reserved for wedding guests. Later in the day they would fly to Tuscany for their honeymoon and I would fly back to London for Wimbledon. Panos's friends were coming and going and telling stories about the reception. Dad walked in.

He came right to us, grabbed the back of a chair from another table with one hand and swept it up to ours. He sat and said to me, "So now do you want to hear about the kid I'm coaching?" There was no hello, no good morning, no congratulations to Panos and Kristie or even an acknowledgment of them at the table. It was direct and aggressive, the way a person would pick a fight.

I looked right at him. What I wanted to say was why don't you go bother someone else. I think my look managed to say that, but I didn't actually speak.

"If not now, when?" he said. "Are you going to dictate to me when I can talk to you?"

Erratic behavior, even for Dad. "Are you still drunk?" He'd always had olive, smooth skin but his face looked puffier than I'd noticed before and he had the beginnings of oysters under his eyes. I wondered how much he'd been smoking and drinking.

"I see. I'm an embarrassment to you. Was I drinking too much last night?"

He was loud and angry. The people in the room were listening and trying hard not to look. "Christ's sake," said Panos.

"Dad, let's take a walk," I said.

"This is it, huh? Big shot calling me out for a fight."

"For a walk, you asshole." I'd never called him an asshole before. Never anything like that. "Let's have this conversation out of the restaurant." I stood. He stood too and we started off without touching each other. I looked back at the table. Kristie looked terrified and was squeezing the hell out of Panos's forearm. He looked worried too. I flashed a palm to say this will be fine.

On the sidewalk Dad and I faced each other square. It was already hot. Philly in the summer has a heavy heat. Cars sped by on Lancaster Avenue. I noticed the pitch of the engine was higher as each car approached, then lower once it passed by and away. The movement of the car compressed or expanded the sound waves depending on where you were standing. I remembered that from eighth-grade physics. I pictured the physics classroom while I stood in front of my deranged father. "What's this all about, Dad?"

"What do you mean?"

"A little aggressive in there. You were rude."

He laughed but it wasn't a real laugh. Just a way to bare his teeth. "They're fine, I wasn't rude. I just want to tell you about this kid. It's impossible to talk to you anymore."

I didn't like talking to him. Not my fault. "Okay, tell me about him."

"What, just like that? Well, sure, but the thing is you really got to go see him play."

"I'm leaving for the airport in thirty minutes."

"I'll send you some video tape."

"What would I do with that? I'm not a coach. I'm working on my own game. I don't understand what you want from me."

His anger rose again. It was clear to us both this had nothing to do with the kid. He said, "Whose side are you on?" He pointed a finger in my chest, pushing into my sternum.

"I'm on my side." I knocked his hand away. It was a hearty smack.

That froze him for a moment. It was the first physical challenge of any kind from me to him. He hadn't expected it. Had never dealt with it before.

In the next moment his instincts took over. He was the silverback and the leadership of his troop had been challenged. That's how he saw it. I wanted to go to London and have nothing more to do with him but he'd gone primal and unconscious.

Rage caused the involuntary transformation of his face that I recognized from my youth. His mind was in an altered state, barely aware of where he was, what he was hearing. He knew only to attack.

I saw the change in his stance, his nostrils, his raised shoulders and fists. I remembered all of it and something triggered in me. Hidden, hurt, angry. Maybe a gene for rampage that he had passed down to me.

We stood face-to-face, committed to whatever came next. It

was a moment bigger than what a psychologist would describe. More for a biologist. It's how species operate and evolve.

When his fists shot forward together toward my chest I was ready. A decade before those fists had launched me backward but now I was wiser. And much bigger.

I rotated my right shoulder back and cocked my fist. My left hand came forward and held his right arm above the elbow. Then my right hand exploded into his face. It felt like I was punching through his head.

He went down in a bush by the restaurant wall and he stayed down. I stood over him and watched the blood spill over his chin to his shirt. His eyes were closed and I watched his sleeping face for a moment then went back inside.

The dining room fell silent when I stepped in. Panos had an arm around Kristie, holding her close.

"Panos, would you get some ice for Dad."

"What happened?"

"He's outside. I hope you two have a great honeymoon. I need to get to the airport." And I left.

37

Neither the Charleston nor Dad's face injured my hand. I was into the second week at Wimbledon and playing well. I looked at the draw of the tournament but spent no time worrying about matchups. I'd take any comers.

The top seeds were all winning that year. I was in the semis, playing the number four seed, a young Croatian guy coached by Ivanisevic. Another tall, lanky left-hander with a big serve, grass specialist and decent on hard courts but lots of holes in his game that made him vulnerable on clay.

He was a threat on grass here at Wimbledon but if I served well I'd have easy holds and would just need to keep taking chances against his serve until I broke him once each set.

That's exactly what I did the first set and won it 6–4. I was executing the plan. It was as certain as mixing chemicals in the lab for a known result. I knew I'd win 6–4, 6–4, 6–4, or better if my opponent gave in.

A day at the office, except there was a fan near Centre Court about ten rows back who was a pain in my ass. It was hard to know if he was for or against me, but he was vocal and loud, and all comments were directed at me. If I hit a winner he'd say something like "That's the way." When I hit an unforced error he'd ride the hell out of me.

I tried to shut out the crowd and didn't want to give him the satisfaction of staring right at him so I took only peripheral, blurred looks. He seemed to be alone and probably drunk. He had a long ZZ Top beard, baseball hat and sunglasses. Big guy too.

He got louder in the second set. He was shouting a running commentary on my play and it was pissing me off. After one outburst I looked at the chair umpire to suggest he might shut the bastard up, but the hollering came between points, not during them, so the umpire felt the guy hadn't yet crossed the line. He made a generic appeal for civility into the loudspeakers.

The fan kept on and got in my head during the points. As I was chasing down balls and hitting strokes my mind would wander to what the next shouts would be. I started to lose more points and the hollering got worse.

After the heckle and my next error I approached the chair. "Can you please get that guy to stop yelling?"

The umpire said into his microphone, "Will the audience please refrain from disturbing the match." He had an English accent which made the warning sound charming and useless. He looked back to me to say that's the extent of what I'm going to do.

I didn't want to show that anything was getting to me and I'd be damned if I was going to double fault the next point so I laid in an easier serve but the Croat walloped it back. A winner up my forehand line.

The caution from the umpire must have only fired the guy up because after this point he stood and yelled, "What the hell kind of serve was that? The women's tour would eat you up!"

A voice loses distinguishing characteristics when in a yell but I could hear that he was American. He reminded me of someone. The devil in one of his disguises. I looked to the umpire who agreed that this was too much. Security was already on the way so I waited at the net by the chair.

Tournament security waved to the guy from the aisle but he wouldn't move. Security moved into the row to assist him by the arm. The guy stood and yelled, "Play the match!"

He was big and he was a problem. The security guard backed off until two more of his colleagues showed up.

My opponent was up at the net with me. He and I and thousands in the stands and millions at home watched the scene play out. A large, maybe drunk, certainly mentally unwell fan brought Wimbledon Centre Court to a halt.

The three security guards moved in. They didn't get rough but they put hands on him, asked him to leave with them. Six more guards arrived in the aisles on either side.

The guy didn't like being touched. He didn't hit but he shook them off. The spectators immediately by him cleared out. It was getting violent.

With one hand he picked up a guard and tossed him forward over a couple rows. The guards from the aisles crashed in.

Two were on his back, two went low and each grabbed a leg. It was like four dogs fighting a bear in a medieval circus. The man fought hard. The hat and sunglasses flew. The beard twisted and ripped off.

Holy shit. Dad.

The loss of disguise seemed to stun him. He stopped putting up a fight and allowed himself to be shoved away, stiff, like a boated marlin staring up from the deck through a lidless eye.

He was gone. The actual tennis match was a distant event and no one knew the way back, least of all me. The stadium was silent, everyone waiting for a voice to fill the air and explain the spectacle.

"Anton," said my opponent. "That was your father?" He knew easily enough. Dad and I had been on the tour a long time. Certainly McEnroe, Carillo, Cahill calling the match from the booth recognized him as well.

It was a private and grotesque moment. Of course I wanted to hide away, pull the curtain over my face, be anywhere but on display. Eyes were on me, cameras were on me recording micro-expressions to be viewed and reviewed for weeks to come. I was conscious enough not to move, to freeze my face, but some facial muscles are involuntary, especially in the moment of surprise. I bounced a tennis ball off the grass to release energy, unfreeze my joints, make sure I could still move. I said, "Yeah. Sorry about that."

The umpire called us back to business. Just like that. There was no injury timeout for mortal humiliation. It was the middle of my service game. I walked back to the baseline giving real thought to defaulting the match, but walking away from the Wimbledon semis would be news as big as Dad rioting in disguise.

I had moments of decent play when the stages of my recovery were anchored in anger but mostly I wanted off the court and I couldn't mount a sustained and serious level of play. I dropped three sets in a row. There was no crowd noise at all the entire way. They all felt a measure of my embarrassment. They didn't want to be there either, as though they felt they were intruding on me despite being paid ticket holders.

I showered with my forehead pressed to the tile, water aimed at the back of my neck as hot as it would go. I was certain they wouldn't fine me for skipping the post-match media event.

In the end I decided to go because that is what is expected, that is what we do. We're creatures of schedules and routines.

I sat behind the cloth-covered folding table, a bottle of water and microphone in front of me. The questions came in a flurry, on top of each other, none about tennis, all about Dad.

Part of me was glad it happened. I could say to them, now do you see? Now do you understand what I've been dealing with?

My mouth had not responded, which made the questions come more furiously, attempts at a rephrase, a new line of inquiry.

I realized it was a mistake to come. I was wounded, raw. I'd say something that revealed too much, make things worse for myself. The press didn't feel they were intruding at all. Cameras clicked and dozens of reporters called out their questions like a pen of excited chickens.

"My dad is not well. Obviously. I'll get him help." I stood and walked out.

38

Within hours of the match I got two phone calls that mattered. The first was Mom.

"Honey, I'm so sorry. Are you okay? I'm so sorry."

"I'm okay."

"Oh, dear God, how could he."

"Where is he?"

"He's on a flight back to Philadelphia now."

"He needs help, Mom."

"I know, it's terrible what he did. He'll see that. He'll feel awful about it."

"I hope you're not asking for sympathy."

"Of course not, I'm sorry. No, it's just that things can get so dark for him. He loves you so much, Anton. He drives himself crazy, he doesn't know what to do about it. He feels shut out."

"Mom, after what you just saw, if you put one bit of this on me, I'm hanging up. For good."

"That's not what I mean. I'm sorry."

"Stop saying that. Stop apologizing."

She choked down another apology and there was silence. "Is there anything I can do for you?"

"That's more like it."

"Oh, honey, I'm sorry. What can I do to help?"

"Nothing, except stop making excuses for him."

"Of course not."

"He needs help."

"I know. Believe me. I want him to get into a better place."

"I don't want him anywhere near me. You tell him that."

"I hope you know how much he loves you, Anton. He's very intense."

I just exhaled. There was a long silence.

"Your father and I are both former athletes. Neither of us knew what to do for a while after our own sports careers. We had you and Panos and I was able to throw myself into mothering two babies. I could do that twenty-four hours a day, seven days a week. He threw himself into his finance career but he never loved it." Incredible. I don't think she even realized she was still making excuses. She couldn't help herself. "By the time Panos and you were in kindergarten and in school to three o'clock I was right back to not knowing how to be an individual. Your father threw himself into you."

"Are you done?"

"I just want you to know that he cares." She was desperate. She wasn't trying to make sense.

"Mom, at this point I don't want to hear about the reasons. I don't want to understand it, don't want to figure out how to deal with it. All that's left anymore is to eliminate it."

"Anton."

"Get him some help. If he comes to another match, ever, I'll get a restraining order and I swear to God, I'll have him thrown in jail."

Two hours later my phone rang again. "Anton, of course I saw. I'm sorry," said Ana.

I was in my hotel in London. I'd tried a movie, food, a book, wine, writing my first-ever journal entry. Everything made me unhappy so after fluttering around the room like an indecisive twit, I was sitting in a dark room imagining I had sunk to the bottom of the ocean for rest. I had booked a flight to Florida for the next day. "Thanks."

"Do you want to talk about it?"

I hadn't heard her voice in nine months. The last time I saw her was the other great shit-show of recent memory, but that didn't matter. Her voice felt good. "Maybe a little."

"Your dad's an obsessive jerk. You've known that."

"True."

"How do you feel?"

Ugh. "Alone. I talked to my mom. Sort of. There's no talking to her really."

"She protects him?"

"It's mind-boggling."

We sat with the phone connecting us for a while, silent, but I was less alone. "Your dad's also a malignant narcissist," she said. "I looked it up."

"Mmm," I said. "About that. Ana, I was out of line."

"We don't need to get into it. Just making a bad joke."

TROPHY SON | 225

There hadn't been any news about Ana and Caleb in months. The last I saw was a photo of them splashing through knee-deep water in St. Barts months ago. Still engaged, still no wedding. "Thanks for letting me off the hook."

"I created a bad situation. Let's leave it there."

"Done," I said. "How's Caleb?" Was that leaving it there? Same guy but different topic, sort of.

"Good, overcommitted. Two films in postproduction, shooting one that's running over and needs to delay the start of the next."

"No time for weddings." Couldn't help that.

"Probably a good thing. The engagement happened in a rush."

I didn't ask directly about second thoughts she might be having. That might have blown up in my face. Or made me sound desperate. And I didn't want to extinguish the glimmer of hope I felt in hearing the doubt in her voice. My masochism again, because I felt we were supposed to be together so I viewed all events as a path to that end, like a lost driver on vaguely familiar roads who thinks each next turn is the one that will put him back on track. On the bright side, Dad was almost entirely out of my mind. "Good to take your time. Be sure about it."

"Yeah."

"He has great hair."

"Mmm-hmm."

"A little short though."

"I'm five-four. Don't be a short-ist."

"How's your writing?"

"It's going well, thanks. Anton, I called to talk to you about you, your dad."

"This is better, trust me. It's helping." She didn't answer right away. Either disbelief or disappointment. "I need to get to the same place you are with parents. Talk on the phone a few times a year. I'm probably there already as of today."

"What I saw today was scary. He has a lot of rage."

"He's a frustrated old man. I punched him, a couple weeks ago. Knocked him out."

"What was the fight about?"

"We were at a wedding. Panos got married. Dad was more obnoxious than usual, either drunk or hungover when I saw him and he picked a fight. Except I've been thinking since that maybe I wanted it, brought it on in a way. Maybe I picked it too."

"I know you, Anton. Pretty well, I think. You choose distance from him over fights with him. But you're strong and stand up for yourself so if he comes after you then there's going to be a fight. You're a good person and I know what you did was okay, and probably sent him the right message."

"The message was to sneak into Wimbledon to start a riot during my match?"

"Your dad needs more time than most to hear the message."

I took a deep breath, sunk into the couch, felt good, warm in my chest. "I miss you." What the hell. Nothing to lose.

"I miss you too." Not mere reciprocity. She thought about that before she said it.

"I'd like to see you."

"Maybe. I don't know."

Damn!

"I can't see you without telling Caleb. That would be," it hung for a moment, "not right."

"I understand."

"Let me think about it."

"Of course."

"Thank you," she said. For what? Patience? She thanked me for something. A masochist would take that as a good sign.

"Thanks for the call, Ana."

Ana didn't get back to me. I had made the stakes pretty high so I shouldn't have expected her to. They didn't break off the engagement but there was still not a wedding announcement, so the length of the engagement was becoming newsworthy.

The next twelve months I played hurt a lot. Nothing major, nothing for the newspapers, just nagging stuff. Sore knees, sore shoulder, sore wrist, temperamental lower back. Sometimes my lower back would seize and cripple me, then Bobby would get some cortisone shots in me to knock back the pain and inflammation and get me back on the court. I was into the second half of my twenties and I noticed recovery was taking a little longer, even with the help from drugs.

I'd skip a tournament to get two weeks off here and there, enough time to rest but not enough to heal. By the third or fourth match back after a two-week break, I'd have the same pains, same cortisone shots. Like a car that's overheating and needs to fully re-set before it can run right again, but I didn't have the time to reset my body. I had to play. I needed tournament points to keep my ranking. If a player doesn't enter enough tournaments in the year, skipping has the same effect as a first-round loss.

I wondered how many of my injuries were the result of the regular wear and tear of an eleven-month season on a 6'3" frame, and how many were the result of my steroid program commanding an unnatural level of performance from my body.

I remembered deaths of old NFL players like Lyle Alzado, some of the Pittsburgh Steelers from the 70s, all the WWF professional wrestlers from the 80s dying off. I had to believe the medicine was a little better now, a little cleaner.

Most of the American guys a few years older than me who played when I was first coming up were all long gone. Rufus Parker hadn't played a professional tournament in two years and was running a tennis camp for teens in San Diego. In tennis, a player can go from kid to veteran in the span of what might be an internship for most industries. And a player can go from a veteran to gone and forgot-ten in the same span of time.

Bobby made small adjustments to my steroid program. Always tweaking, optimizing, keeping me at the maximum. We'd com-mitted to that for a few more years, as long as I could stay at the top of the game. Money was coming to me from places I'd never imagined before.

Of course the prize money was good and the sports apparel en-dorsements were great, and that I expected. But my agent also got money deals for me on fragrances, watches, private airlines, clothing labels, cars. I never did much for any of these deals. I just allowed my agent to tell people they could use my name, and they paid me. What my agent called "passive income." It was more than my prize money.

There was a lot invested in staying on top of the game. My body was reminding me all the time that my run at number one would be finite and that my run in the game at all wouldn't be much longer than the time at number one. I didn't feel a slow decline coming on. I felt a collapse, like the snapping of a rope bridge over a canyon.

I also increased the amount of alcohol I drank during my two-week mini-breaks. I dated no one seriously. Tennis was a sentence and I needed to serve my time first and until then I'd make do with the company I could find.

I was in my New York apartment drinking beer with Adam on a mini-break when Gabe called my phone. I muted the TV and tried to sound sober. "Hey, Gabe."

"Anton, we have a problem."

Gabe was never dramatic. He didn't talk that way so I stood up as a reflex, which reminded me how drunk I was. "What's up?"

Adam looked over since the TV was muted.

Gabe said, "You got flagged. BB&T Atlanta Open. The test came back positive."

"Bullshit. That's not possible." I sounded drunk since I was starting to panic and forgetting to try to sound sober. "Gabe, I don't flag these, ever." My brain was scrambling. In calm moments, I've wanted out of tennis plenty of times, but now this felt like a death sentence. First humiliation, then death, and I was having a physical reaction to the news. My heart was pounding more blood into my skull than the veins there could handle and I was out of breath. "Could there be a mix-up? Did they make a mistake?"

"No, it's no mistake, it's too far down the path. I spoke to the lawyer for the ITF. They've checked and rechecked."

"How the fuck did this happen?" I was still standing, walking now, and Adam stood too.

"I don't know. Maybe they started using a different agent in the test, maybe Bobby tried something new he shouldn't have."

"Fucking Bobby."

"Let's pick this up when we get together in person."

That was code for shut-the-hell-up-about-your-steroid-program while talking on the phone, just in case, and I was sober enough to get it. "Fine."

"There's a bit of good news," he said.

It took me a moment but I circled the room back to the sofa, sat, and said, "What?"

"Well, the thing is, you're the number one player in the world."

"So what?"

"That gives you some leverage, even in a situation like this."

"What do I do?"

"You won't have to do anything, other than say yes to what I expect will be a pretty sweet deal. Under the circumstances."

"What's the deal?"

"He wouldn't say, but we have a meeting. Tomorrow. In New York."

We met at Keens Steakhouse in Midtown at 11:30am the next day. The lunch crowd hadn't come yet so there were only a few waiters getting ready and a hostess in front. The restaurant was dark with low ceilings and stretched far back like a cave.

The hostess was expecting us and took us in a different direction, up a flight of stairs then turned right and opened a set of heavy double doors.

"Your party is here. Welcome to the Theodore Roosevelt Room."

Two men stood at the far side of a huge, round table that could seat twenty-five. One was tanned with black hair and a trim tailored, bright-blue suit with a purple tie. He said, "Anton, Gabe, thank you for coming. Come in, come in." He had a Spanish accent. He came around the table to shake our hands and lead us to two seats at the table, leaving one seat of space between us and them.

"Of course," said Gabe.

"My apologies," said the man. "I didn't know this table would be so absurd for our purposes today, but I wanted a private room and this surely will be private."

There were old tobacco pipes and animal heads hung around the walls. I stayed standing and speechless. I was nervous. I was a convict waiting for my sentencing to be read.

"My name is Chi Chi Ruiz. I serve as the Executive Vice President of the International Tennis Federation. My office is in the London headquarters." He had a smile full of very white teeth, he was happy, relaxed, like we were all here for a social lunch. He put a hand on the shoulder of the man in a charcoal suit next to him. "This is Alan Eberhart with Couchman Harrington Associates, the law firm that we keep on retainer. It's necessary that Alan be here today," he said by way of apology.

"Hello," said Alan. He was so curt it was hard for an accent to work its way into the syllables but I detected British.

He shook hands with two pumps for each me and Gabe, then sat, so then we all sat too. I still hadn't said a word.

Chi Chi said, "Thanks again for coming," which was a silly

thing to say. It wasn't a favor. I had to come. "We all know the unfortunate reason we're here and Alan and I have come all the way to New York so we can handle this situation in a way that is best for the ITF, best for you, best for the game of tennis, best for the fans of the game of tennis. Now, I have to tell you, this is a highly political issue within the ITF leadership, but over the last week we've worked out some ideas for moving forward. Alan will take us through the basics." Gabe and I were scared, Alan seemed angry. Chi Chi turned to Alan with a lunatic smile.

Alan started, "By way of background," he had the tone of reading text he hated, "in 1993 the ITF and ATP began the Joint Anti-Doping Programme. In 2006 the ITF took control of the programme for the men's tour and in 2007 for the women's tour as well. The ITF handles all drug testing at ITF-sponsored events, including the Grand Slam events, as well as all ATP-sanctioned events." He paused. "The ITF is the governing body for drug testing." This sounded very much like a threat.

"So you just deal with us," said Chi Chi, putting on a positive spin.

Alan ignored him and continued in official speak, "On July thirty-first of this year, at the BB&T Atlanta Open, the ITF conducted a routine post-match drug test of Anton Stratis. The testing detected banned substances." He paused and shuffled a new paper to the top of his stack. "Mr. Stratis, the test detected three banned substances. First, diuretics, a banned substance commonly used to help the body lose fluids and mask the presence of other drugs. Second, beta-2 agonists, a banned substance commonly used to relax smooth muscle around the lungs, enabling greater lung capacity and higher performance. Third, anabolic steroids, a banned substance commonly used to build muscle and speed physical recovery."

I wished Bobby was there so he could also receive the failing grade personally. Our enormous room and enormous table were all quiet for a moment, then Chi Chi laughed. Through his laughter he said, "It really was a spectacular failure, Anton. I mean big-time." He shook his head. "So here we are. Our head clinician, Dr. Miller, ventured a guess that the diuretic in your program failed. It showed up present in your test but didn't mask anything."

I nearly thanked him for the gratuitous analysis.

Gabe said, "If we appeal?"

"Let's not get ahead of ourselves," said Chi Chi, keeping the floor from Alan. "I've looked at this from a lot of angles. I pushed for a Therapeutic Use Exemption but there was no support for me on that. Back-dating an application for a TUE from you would be tricky, and there has been no apparent injury or media coverage of an injury to support the claim. Plus if it ever got out which substances came up in the test, that wouldn't line up either." He raised his hands. "The point is, I'm trying to help you."

"That doesn't answer my question," said Gabe.

"Gabe, you're dead to rights," said Chi Chi. "There's no appeal. That would be just a big media circus, and nobody wants that."

Gabe nodded.

Chi Chi said, "But there's good news in all of that, if you listen to exactly what I just said. Nobody wants a big media circus!" He looked from Gabe, now to me. "You're the number one fucking player in the world!" He sounded like Raul Julia. "That's the point of leverage I've been working on your behalf."

Alan looked frustrated and I realized Chi Chi was a rogue operator trying to handle this in a way that made lawyers squirm. He wanted my test gone as much as I did. Not because he liked me personally. He liked that I sold tickets and TV rights and tennis needed a clean image to keep growing revenue.

I still hadn't heard my sentence issued and I didn't feel ready to speak. Gabe said, "Where did that leverage get us?"

"Well, again, this is highly political," said Chi Chi. "We don't want our number one player out on a drug ban. But we can't just do nothing either. That won't fly. The ITF leadership is clear that they won't hand out a pass on this. So where does that leave us? How do we satisfy both?"

Gabe and I looked at each other. I had the feeling he was right that we might get a sweet deal.

"A six-month suspension," said Chi Chi. He looked back and forth at us both trying to gauge a reaction. Gabe and I stayed stone faced. "But we won't call it a suspension. There's no need to label it. As a practical matter, you will not play for six months. Release a statement about some injury, make something up that takes six months to heal. Take some time off." He smiled his biggest yet. "So you do six months. Call it a vacation, call it a suspension. What's in a name?"

Gabe and I looked at each other. I was thrilled. I knew Gabe was too. This was the best outcome he had hoped for but he was savvy enough not to look thrilled in front of them. "Six months is a long time," he said.

Chi Chi looked annoyed for the first time. "Gabe, this is a gift and you know it." His comments were all directed to Gabe. "You know we have to come down with some punishment. I'm saving your athlete's neck here. It's six months, and that overlaps December which is a month out anyway, so you're really looking at five. You can keep training, quietly, off the radar. Anton keeps his reputation, all that nice money coming in on the side. And tennis avoids a black eye."

"Well," said Gabe.

Chi Chi pointed a finger at Gabe. I could see he had plenty of fire behind the smile. He had been sent here to sew this up, make sure we cooperated. "You need to work with me on this, Gabe. It's the best deal you'll get. Take it now, as is, or I promise your life and Anton's life will turn to shit."

Gabe looked at me and nodded. I nodded back then said to Chi Chi, "Alright." My one and only word of the meeting.

The group's focus returned to Alan who said, "This is a verbal understanding between the parties. For a period of six months, commencing today, Anton Stratis agrees that he will not enter any ITF- or ATP-sanctioned event, nor will he play tennis in public in any way that demonstrates he is at full physical health during the six-month period. Should you apply for entry to any event your application will be rejected. The ITF reserves the right to publish the drug test results in the future if it feels in its own judgment that Anton Stratis has not fulfilled this agreement in good faith."

Chi Chi was smiling again. "Call it a wrist injury. Show up to play again in six months, wear a brace, put a little mascara on it. Enjoy some vacation, then boom, boom, boom, you're back in."

40

I couldn't sleep well. One thing I'd always been able to do with excellence and consistency was sleep, but that skill had left me literally overnight. I became like an upset octogenarian who complains he can never get more than a few hours snooze at a time.

My youthful battles with OCD had shifted to hours of staring at the ceiling in a dark room, wandering mind, hallucinating eyes, trying warm milk, trying warm milk with bourbon, getting up to pee six times and returning to bed each time with a new configuration and body contortions, like running on a treadmill that moved me back farther from sleep the faster I tried to run toward it. By the middle of the night I was the most alert and crazed I'd be in a twenty-four-hour period.

The daytime would be shot. I'd muddle through a workout with Gabe then take a nap which would certainly condemn me to another night of hell.

It started exactly when my sentence began. My absence. I could call it neither a vacation nor a suspension, so when the team needed to make reference to that six-month period, we'd taken to calling it my absence.

Parts of the absence were okay. My body was healing, proving that the damage I'd done wasn't yet permanent. My back didn't seize, my knees didn't ache. I could stretch my muscles, move without pain.

Though as my body came back to me, new mental battles began. This was my first taste of what the end would be like. It was only a faux ending. I knew I'd play again and needed to train, but it was six months to relax with no match pressure. I had days in a row away from the court and the gym. Ninety-six hours sometimes.

Professional athletes are handed a schedule with greater detail than that for a head of state. I didn't need to decide what to eat and how much, when to go to the gym, for how long and what to do there, when to go to the tennis court and which battery of drills, how many more calories for fuel, how much free time, when to go to bed, when to wake back up and do it again.

It's not that I had no say. I took advice from Gabe and Bobby, but I had all the say. It was a system and the good thing about systems was they took out variability because you never had to decide anything. The bad thing was when the system went away. I had to wake up in the morning and decide everything. I had no ability to structure my own day. I was lucky to feed myself on the days I didn't train.

At night I would lie in bed and think about what kind of future this would be for me. I'd think about Joe Montana. How did he relearn to structure his time without a coach blowing whistles at him, giving him a playbook and workout regimen, a locker room complete with teammates and a community that wouldn't and couldn't leave him?

So that would keep me awake and I'd try the trick to empty my head for sleep by saying, "Nothing, nothing, nothing," over and over again and I thought, how fucking ironic. That's exactly what I'm afraid of.

At 2am Eastern Standard Time, I called her phone, not knowing where on the planet she was. "You awake?"

"Hey, yes," said Ana. "You okay?"

She already knew about my steroid use so I told her all about my suspension-vacation-absence. "I have a greater understanding of assisted living. Why shuffleboard and bingo are so popular."

"Bored?"

"Something a few degrees beyond that." Want to come visit Florida, I thought, then said, "Where are you?"

"Toronto." Still engaged, still no wedding.

Different country, same time zone though. "I woke you?"

"I was getting up in six hours anyway."

"What's going on in Toronto?"

"Film festival. I had a role in a picture that we entered here. A few press appearances to do here and there, otherwise just goofing around."

Please ask me, please ask me. "Sounds like a good time. Toronto's a fun town."

Then it came. "Would you like to come up? Check it out?" She even sounded a little nervous. The good kind, like she was worried I'd say no. "Put all your free time to something useful."

"Right. Take in some culture." I felt sleep might come after this call. "I'll look at flights. Dinner tomorrow night?"

I had a car meet me at the Toronto airport to drive directly to The Forth, a restaurant on the east end of the city, to meet Ana, and I texted her that I had landed and was on the way. It was the first time in my life I'd flown alone. It was a nice feeling. Like I was skipping class, getting away with something.

Toronto's a cosmopolitan city and The Forth was a fancy place. I picked it because it had authentic Canadian food. Whatever that means.

The hostess took me right to the table so I could wait for Ana there. I wasn't big on fancy restaurants but the people in them tend to leave you alone. I sipped a gin and tonic until Ana arrived. It occurred to me that the last time I dropped in on a woman I cared so much about, things did not go well.

She trailed the hostess, weaving to our table, to me. There was no football punter attached to her backside. As she approached, waves of diners stopped moving and stared, like a rolling blackout across a city, until the entire restaurant was frozen, watching her walk to the table where I stood and kissed her lips, something I'd decided to do during the gin and tonic. Let them write about it in the blogs.

Ana kissed me back as though this was how we greeted each other. Dinner was off to a good start.

Ana saw my gin and tonic, decided it looked good and ordered one for herself. I liked when a date copied my drink order. It signaled she trusted me, felt safe in my hands.

"You look good," she said. "Some time away from the tennis tour seems to agree with you."

I'd gained five pounds and probably did look healthier. "There's plenty of room for agreement," I said, "with some adjustment."

"You wouldn't be bored for long. You can't really move on now because you're going to play again. When it's time to really move on, you will."

I raised my glass in a toast to that remark and drank. "How's the festival?"

"It's been fun, a lot of friends are here. Some good pictures and ours is getting some good reviews. Might pick up an award."

"Congratulations. Have you had a chance to see some of the other pictures?"

"Yes, most of them."

"Which are the good ones?"

She leaned back and laughed, sipped her drink then returned it to the table. "Don't small-talk me, Anton. You flew to Toronto. Out with it."

She was dynamite. "You invited me to Toronto."

"All the more reason that it's your turn."

So it was time to lay it out there. "Look, I . . . You know I've cared for you, I think I've loved you, for a long time. With your schedule and my schedule, we'd see each other a few weeks a year, even if you were a roadie with me between your pictures, which is a bad idea, that's the best we'd do. So I've always convinced myself that it's a bad idea, that we'd take something that could be good and we'd ruin it by forcing impossible circumstances."

I waited a moment, giving her a chance to say something, but she watched me.

"I also had a bad experience with a girl when I was young and maybe that makes me a little tentative."

"How bad?"

"Bad, humiliating. Another guy." That was all I would say about Liz until we were old and gray. "But now I don't want to wait anymore. I might play two more years, three at the most. I'd be free of tennis then, but I don't want to be a slave to it even that long. I love you and I want that part of my life to start. It gets down to what I said already. I don't want to wait anymore."

"I'm engaged."

She had tears in her eyes. This was either very good or very bad and it was unfair to us both to leave it unresolved. "Ana, I'm going to get up, walk to the bathroom. I'll linger there a few minutes. When I get back, if you're gone, you should know that you'll always have a special place in my heart and I wish you well. I'm happy I've had the chance to know you. If, when I get back, you're still here, I'll know there's a chance for us."

I stood. Seemed like a good plan but my legs were unsteady. I walked to the bathroom with my arms forward and to the sides for balance as though holding ski poles. I didn't look back.

In the bathroom I bent over the sink and splashed my face, then gripping the sides of the sink and still bent forward I looked up at my reflection, so close I could see the capillaries in the whites of my eyes. I asked what kind of a life are you going to have, Anton? There are butterfly effects that lead to sliding doors, massive determinations in our lives due to faraway forces. We can't live our lives paying attention to these forces because they are tiny or even unknown, and they're constant. But this was the tempest, right here, right now.

I closed my eyes, counted to one hundred eighty, frozen over the sink while the bathroom attendant stared and wondered if he needed to call the manager. At one-eighty I stood straight, fixed my hair, took a deep breath. "Please be there."

The men's room was down a short corridor from the dining room. I could see the exact tile in the floor where I'd have my first view of our table. I started to regret what I'd done. Why did I put that pressure on her? It was unnatural.

I got to the tile, stopped, didn't look. Salvation or execution? Not the healthiest way to look at things, but that's how it felt at the time. I looked over. Two half-full gin and tonics, tiny flower arrangement, candle, flatware, salt, pepper. No Ana. She was gone. Of course she was.

I stood there like a fool, watching the empty chairs, hoping the view would change. I felt sick and couldn't possibly eat. Maybe I could put some cash on the table for the drinks and the time and sneak out.

A hand came around my waist from behind, then another and a body pressed close against me. Ana whispered, "I'm right here."

I turned, not understanding, still too deep in the other emotions. I looked her in the eye. "You're still here," I repeated her.

She laughed. "Yes."

I hugged her into me. "Thank God."

41

My first tournament back was Houston and Ana travelled with me. She wasn't with me in the way that new and infatuated couples can't be apart. She was with me in the way that couples of many years develop an instinct for when their partner needs support.

Houston is a smaller tournament, which I preferred for my return. It was played on clay, which I did not prefer.

Ana had slipped out of bed so I could sleep and she was drinking coffee, reading the paper in the next room of our hotel suite. I opened my eyes and unfolded my arm across the bed where she had been. It was 9am and I'd slept for ten hours.

I slid my legs off the side. "Good morning."

Ana stepped into the frame of the bedroom doorway wearing an open robe held apart by her breasts and showed blue panties for a bit of color. "You sleep as well as a nine-month-old."

"Only when things are right."

She knew I didn't drink coffee so she carried a bottle of water to me. She straddled my hips, pushing me back on the bed and leaned over me so we were both inside her robe, her warm skin on mine. "After your match today, I'm going to have sex with you."

"The tennis tour is so much more fun than it used to be."

I won my match that day. I was physically fresh, mentally rusty and would have lost to a top-ten player. I had great sex with Ana back in the hotel after, reckless, insatiable for each other, moving from room to room, then resting, napping on each other like cats, then sex again.

Ana's presence at the tournament announced our couple-dom. That same day, the *Entertainment Tonight* website had named us Anaton and pronounced her engagement to Caleb Casa officially dead.

We ordered room service for dinner rather than go out and I said, "I'm sorry there isn't more for you to do here this week."

"Don't be, this is perfect. I get to watch great tennis from the player's box, I'm getting some writing done, and I'm with you."

"You have a life to get back to."

"It's a week. There's no place in the world I'd rather spend this week."

I cupped my hands around her jaw and kissed her forehead.

She said, "I want to be with you and I can be here without any problem. In a few years it'll be your turn. You'll have to sit in a Broadway theater watching play rehearsals."

"I can't wait." I dropped my hands. "When I retire, there are no more tournaments on grand stages, first-class travel, fancy parties with fancy people. I'm just another guy without a high school diploma."

"That's exactly the person I want to get to know better."

My second-round match was a terrible grind. He was a left-handed Spanish player, veteran, great on clay, steady as hell. Every game seemed to go to deuce, back and forth. I had moments of playing like my best self but that's never enough. Tons of guys can play great for moments.

Each set went to a tiebreaker. I'd have flashes of great stuff to go up, then he kept coming, staying with me, drawing even then taking the lead. My body was still strong, willing, needing a leader to guide it, but my mind was still not tournament sharp.

I lost to this Spanish veteran who had barely taken games off me in our three previous meetings. I was less than I had been before but he was also more. I wondered what steroid program he was on.

In my months away from the tour Ben Archer had taken over the number one ranking. He'd been hovering around the top five for a few years, then put together a strong half season that put him in the top spot. I had mixed emotions because I liked Ben, but it felt unjust to me that after everything I'd been through, a lesser player on emotional cruise control could accomplish the same, leave the same legacy that I had feared would elude me, a legacy that I had felt desperate to establish because I needed something to show for all the hell of it.

In the hotel room I said, "I hope you weren't falling in love with Houston."

"Paris in a couple months sounds good."

"I'll be playing better by then."

"I know you will."

"The saying goes, you don't need to be the best player every day, you just need to be better than the one guy across the net.

Couldn't do it today." I hated losing. I hated talking about a loss. Having Ana with me was one more reason to stop both.

"It was your first tournament back."

I nodded. "I still have some great tennis in me." I kissed her. "Let's pack."

42

A player's will has endurance that can be trained and conditioned. The will can get in poor condition more easily than the body. I made the semis in each of the remaining three majors my first season back. It was a decent showing because I was able to feed off the energy of the large stage.

It was the smaller tournaments where I struggled to keep my intensity. When people talk about mental toughness and a test of wills between players, that's not just something to say. There's an invisible battle in every match, simultaneous with the points played with a racket.

Even in a match that ends in victory a player might lose more than a hundred points. That's a hundred points that didn't go your way, ended in disappointment, that you need to bounce back from immediately and play on at your best. If a player can't do that every single time, whole games slip away, whole sets, whole matches. It's really damn hard. Damn tedious.

I was back in Atlanta of all places. Ana wasn't with me. What should have been an easy forehand winner up the line I sent two feet wide. The miss angered me. Fatigued me, at the thought of the hole I'd needlessly dug for myself in that game. I went on to lose the next point, then the game, then the set.

My mental state was exhausted, worn out. I had the mental fragility of my teenage years, but with more firepower to mask it. With my firepower failing, I had the horrible thought return from my youth: Kill me quickly. I disappeared from the match in a way that I hadn't done since before turning pro. I lost 6–0 in the final set.

I could feel the physical wear and tear of the season on my body more than ever, though if I wanted to get the number one ranking back, it was more important that I get my head in shape. But my willingness to suffer was almost gone.

I went to the locker room by myself. I'd talk with Gabe after the press conference and a shower. I dropped my racket bag then slumped into a cushioned chair. At twenty-eight and as a former number one, I was an elder statesman in the locker room. Other than a "Hi, Anton," people spoke with me only after I spoke with them first. There was a general feeling that any player after reaching number one could be as bad a diva as Jimmy Connors.

I sat in silence, letting my mind rest, heal from the injury it had just suffered. My eyes were open, looking through the floor at nothing. Players went about their routines around me, maybe glancing, knowing it was better to leave me be.

In a moment, two bright white tennis sneakers came into my view and stopped in front of me. I followed the legs up to the stomach, chest and face to see Martin Sage, a former player turned coach.

Martin was an American who retired around the time I first came on the tour. Early forties now, coaching a young Australian kid who had good talent. Martin had been a top-twenty player himself for long stretches in his career.

"Nice sneakers," I said.

"Haven't seen much action yet."

"I guess not."

"Take a walk?"

I knew Martin a bit. We'd had maybe four conversations in ten years. None of them was over a walk so it was odd, but I thought what the hell. "Sure."

He reached out a hand and lifted me up from the chair. There was a back door from the locker room that led to a player's entrance from the parking lot behind a security checkpoint. Plenty of people could see us but nobody was closer than thirty yards. We stopped there and Martin said in a normal conversational volume, "How are you?"

"Shitty. What kind of question is that?"

He laughed. "I'm sorry. I meant bigger picture."

"I'm alright," I said.

He nodded and waited awhile before talking again. "I don't know you that well, Anton, but I've always liked you. Always thought you were a class act."

Martin was a respected guy around the tour, especially among Americans. He hadn't been a star player but everyone liked him. "Thanks, Martin."

"You can still play some great tennis if you want to. Dominant tennis."

"I think so too."

"Take it from a retired guy. The window slams shut very fast.

People think their babies grow up too fast. They should try having a professional tennis career."

"Clock's ticking, I know." The advice was a little condescending but coming from a good place and somehow I didn't mind it.

"Make what you can of it, my man. I'm rooting for you." He clapped my shoulder. "So you're dating Ana Stokke? How's it going?"

"Is that rhetorical? It's fantastic, of course." Martin was single and known to be a ladies' man.

He laughed again. He laughed easily. Maybe retirement was okay. "Well, hang on to her."

"You bet."

The laugh faded out and I realized it came easily because it had little substance, was hollow, nearly weightless, only a cover. "I mean it. Hang on for dear life. Not an expression. Hang on."

This was weird enough that I changed the subject. "How's coaching going?"

"It's good, you know?" he said. "It's good to be around the game. Maybe I'll make a run at the announcers' booth one day if I can get McEnroe to back me. Anyway, you know the deal. What the hell else are we going to do?"

I wasn't ready to sign on for that. I feared it, but still had hopes of a second act of Anton, a second life that was me and not tennis, but I didn't want to say any of that to Martin so I said, "Right."

Some fans screamed to us from the ticket-holders parking lot. I looked over and several were taking pictures with their phones. I waved.

Martin waved too and smiled. He said, "If you're going to die at age thirty-five, professional sports is the best life ever. If you're going to die at eighty-five, it's the worst. The best life ever lived by anyone in any walk of life was Lou Gehrig."

43

I won the Doha tournament in Qatar to start the next calendar year. The Qatar ExxonMobil Open. The tournament drew top players and it was a solid win for me so I was surprised I didn't feel more of an emotional lift.

Ana was with me. Qatar was one of the more fun destinations so she shifted her schedule for me and got to do some sightseeing, ride Arabian horses. I was physically beat up after the final so we celebrated the win with wine and room service in our hotel suite.

Ana said, "You look exhausted."

Something a woman can say to a man but not the other way around. "I feel it," I said.

She poured the wine. My back was killing me and I couldn't sit comfortably. Bobby had given me a cortisone shot after the match but I was still in pain. Ana carried some pillows over then stood by me not knowing where to put them.

"I think the best position is if I just sit up as straight as I can."

"This better not affect our sex life."

"We'll find a way." In the morning Ana would fly back to New York and I would fly to Melbourne. "Or I'll quit."

She poured more wine. "You can't quit now. I'm just beginning to enjoy being a tennis roadie."

I smiled. "I'm almost done."

She looked at me wondering if we were still joking or if I had turned serious. She said, "Don't make tennis decisions based on me. Truly, I'm fine. I'm okay doing this for a while."

This communicated a lot to me. The words and the tone. She loved me, but this was a system that wouldn't last. Not more than a year or so. "Well, I'm almost done anyway. For lots of reasons."

"You're playing great tennis."

"That stopped mattering to me. Playing great matters only when it makes you happy. Borg was playing great when he quit. He just stopped wanting to play anymore." I drank my wine and tried standing up to relieve my back. "Maybe I've done everything I set out to do in tennis. I made it to number one, I won a major, I made plenty of money. I met you." She was seated and I kissed the top of her head. "Now it's drive for the sake of drive. More winning, more winning, build the résumé, the legacy. As my father would do it."

"You're very different from your father."

"But I've internalized him as my tormentor. This wasn't what I chose, but here I am on my own and choosing it, every day, pushing myself as hard as he did." I twisted and untwisted my spine in a stretch. "At least I'm doing the pushing, it's a willful act, but what does that say about me?"

"That you're a champion, that you demand excellence of yourself. There's nothing wrong with that. Your father pushed you into tennis so you made the most of it, and you'll make the most of whatever you decide to do next."

"Maybe I'm becoming the monster. I'm my own monster now, and what if I have a son or a daughter? And I'm irreparably a monster?"

I felt certain I would not push my imagined kids too hard but be kind and loving and if anything would overcompensate and be too soft. But maybe it would be an instinct I couldn't resist or even identify, like people who complain about angry soccer sideline parents and then become them. Ana said what I'd hoped she'd say. "That's outrageous."

"Maybe not."

"If you want to quit because winning tournaments doesn't make you as happy as it used to, then fine. But don't quit because you think you're transforming into a beast."

I hadn't had the same feeling about tennis since I'd come back from the suspension. This was the same period when Ana and I had gotten together so it was hard to know if the change was due to the time away or if Ana had given me a window to what a life away from tennis could be, or if it was just that I was in more physical pain at that age.

My world ranking was back up to four. The next spots were always the hardest to make up but I wanted to do it. I wanted to get to number one or win another major, then say good-bye.

44

I finally had some time in my New York apartment before travelling to play Cincinnati. Ana was also in New York but her new play was running four weeks of preview performances at the Ethel Barrymore on Broadway before opening night so she was there every evening.

I went to the downstairs bar at the Gramercy Hotel with some other players who were decompressing for a few days in the city. Adam came with us. Some of the big-name female players would travel with security but on a social night I was always fine if just a few friends came along for insulation.

The downstairs at Gramercy was a huge, open square room with comfortable chairs and sofas that created different conversation pods. Security at the door was selective about the people they let inside but they knew we were coming and one of the guys in a suit and earpiece led Adam and me back into the bar lounge.

Darren Rose was one of the guys meeting us. He was thirty-six, one of the oldest on tour, and still a top doubles player. He'd always been a doubles specialist. Big guy, about 6'6", big serve, monster at net. He had blond surfer hair that took a few years off his appearance and he could pass for Laird Hamilton. Darren was with Toby McInerny, another doubles player.

They were sitting in a square with three sofas that had been cordoned off by the same red velvet rope used outside. The enclave made a spectacle of us but gave us a buffer. A hotel security guard unclipped the rope from a corner post and waved us in. There were about a hundred people in the room outside our square watching us.

"Come in, gentlemen," said Darren. He gestured to a coffee table in the middle of the sofas where he'd ordered bottle service. There was a liter of Ketel One vodka, carafes of orange juice, cranberry, club soda and a bowl of lemons, limes and orange wedges.

"Don't mind if I do," said Adam.

We sat and Adam made two vodka sodas for us.

"Where's your super-hot girlfriend?" said Darren.

"Working. Directing a new play she wrote."

"She might have had the courtesy to send a few friends in her stead." Darren liked to talk smart, as though it was a skill and benefit that came with being thirty-six.

There were several very good-looking girls, and maybe some hookers, watching our group. "I don't think you'll have any trouble tonight."

"I guess not," said Darren. He looked over at two girls in miniskirts who had been looming by our red rope. They were attractive enough to reasonably expect an invitation in, and Darren said, "Ladies, come have a drink." He nodded to the security guard who unclipped the rope then clipped it again behind them. They slotted into the sofa with Darren and Toby and paired up easily as though all were following stage direction. Toby fixed four new drinks then each girl nestled under the wing of a doubles player.

"Don't let me hold you back," I said to Adam. He knew I wouldn't mess around on Ana, nor did I want a photo of a girl on my arm to go around the Internet.

"I'd like to have a drink or two first." He clinked my glass. "To Cincinnati."

"Don't remind me."

I looked at Darren. I liked him. He was one of those guys with a big personality, always smiling, always having fun, always with something to say, never complaining. He was harmless. Unless you were a girl who expected things might end differently. Or you were the husband or boyfriend of the girl. I suppose the thing is he meant no harm.

But I saw him differently in that moment, past the surfer hair and the still-hard muscles of a professional athlete. I saw for the first time the wrinkles around his eyes and mouth, his worry, regret, as though the oils of his Dorian Gray painting were oozing back into him.

He looked old to me. Seated next to the fresh, young and pliant girls he looked old and pathetic. Desperate for their youth. I saw more fear in his eyes than I did in the timid and wondering eyes of the girls.

I remember video clips of Patrick Ewing running the floor in his last NBA season. He looked like a lame dinosaur and it hurt my own knees just to watch him. He was one of the greats but he'd stayed too long.

Darren looked the same to me. Not in any physical way, and he could still play great. Just that he was out of place. He shouldn't have been here, but I knew why a guy like that stayed. Not the money. Not even the game. It was the lifestyle.

And that's the irony. The sick truth of it, for any top player, for any child prodigy gone pro, for me and my relationship with tennis.

We hung on to this thing that crippled our humanity because now that our humanity was crippled, this thing was all that we believed could make us happy anymore.

I got cortisone shots about once a tournament. I could sit in one position about five minutes before my back would start to hurt. "Atom Bomb, you look bored," said Adam.

"Just relaxing."

Adam put more ice, vodka and soda in my glass while I held it. I pulled a long sip and thought about the differences over ten years. I used to live and travel with Dad, a late-teen player with promise, known to a few people deep in tennis circles. Now I was in an exclusive Manhattan lounge, perched on a sofa behind a square of red rope like a museum exhibit. I'd earned a fortune and millions of people knew my name, my face and something of my story. I was dating a famous actress. All enviable stuff.

People in that bar would be surprised to learn that I spent any time fearing what came next for me. But the fact is that every person is fighting a battle we might know nothing about. Minkoff helped me identify my battle years earlier. I was specialized. My battle was to be a whole man.

Adam had managed primitive, nonverbal communications with a great-looking girl who was loitering by the security guard. She came through the unclipped rope led by her breasts six inches ahead of the rest of her. Adam was delighted and fixed her a vodka cranberry. Her voice was breathy and affected like a 1940s Hollywood star.

I said a pleasant hello and was relieved when she shared our sofa on the other side of Adam so I could lean back in seclusion.

I thought to myself that all Americans should go out at the US Open. It was the last major of the season and it was New York City. A player should see it through to there, then retire.

I saw a T-shirt once that read "New York Fucking City." That said it all.

I'd be twenty-nine by this year's US Open. It seemed like the right time to do it. I'd stopped waiting for Ana and I could stop waiting for everything else just by deciding to make it so. I finished my drink with a second long sip and wondered if I'd feel the same after I woke in the morning, after I'd spoken with Ana. Were these decisions real or would these be like the vows of a drunkard?

In twenty minutes more I bid my friends good luck on their adventures and went home to meet Ana who would soon be there.

That night I slept well. I had fallen off before Ana got home from her play. In the morning we rolled on our sides to face each other.

"How was the play?"

"Almost entirely smooth for the first time. The kinks are out."

"Good." I took her hand. "My mind wandered into a couple decisions last night and I want to run two things by you."

"Yikes."

"Maybe. Hopefully not." She was stretched long and sideways with her head resting in her hand supported by her elbow on the mattress and her eyes looked huge and beautiful. "I don't need a yes, but I need to know these are not deal-breakers for you."

"Still yikes."

I laughed and sat up. "I want kids. Some day."

"Okay."

"Deal-breaker or not a deal-breaker?"

"Not a deal-breaker."

I squeezed her hand. "That's one. One to go."

"So far, not yikes."

"I want to retire at the US Open."

"The one in one month or the one in thirteen months?"

"One month."

"When your mind wanders, it doesn't mess around."

"It feels right."

When I was on the tour I had little time for relationships outside tennis and people had to work harder to stay in my life. Panos did what he could but was mainly there as an example of what a happy life could be. Successful financial advisor, house in the suburbs, kid on the way, happy wife, good enough at tennis to win championships at the country club. Not for me, but not bad at all.

Ana didn't say "And then what." She knew I would go after whatever was the next thing and that for now we were together so we could go after it as partners and see if we could make our partnership work too. She said only, "Great. I'm in."

I didn't want a whole season with my retirement pre-announced, sentimental good-byes at each tournament. I wanted it quick like this. I called Gabe, Bobby, Adam, the only team I'd ever had as a pro, and I told them. Gabe called press contacts and told them. And so it was announced. Anton Stratis would be out of tennis by a week after Labor Day.

45

Everyone I passed spoke to me that time at the US Open. Security guards, ushers, caterers, tour officials. They all said things like "This is your tournament, Anton," "Get one more," "Thanks for all the great tennis over the years." It felt damn nice and made me think that a little bit of a child's game is what a grown person needs. I touched a lot of lives and though I was only a diversion from their own battles, I touched them in a positive way.

I was playing well and holding up physically. I got through to the semifinal and dropped only one set in a tiebreaker. I lost only two service games in four matches.

I was to play the world number one in the semis. Erik Gerhardt, a twenty-five-year-old English kid who'd held the number one ranking for three months. He had thick legs like Gabe but he was 6'4" and a bull, fast and physical like Boris Becker.

I'd faced him twice before and I won both times. He'd taken on Patrick McEnroe as his new coach which had lifted his game, but I still didn't consider him all that dangerous a player. He was the reigning number one but he wouldn't go down as an all-time great. He was a very good player who'd been playing great the way Lleyton Hewitt did for a while.

I was the first semifinal match which meant I had a certain start time and didn't have to wait around for another match. The tournament sends Mercedes SUVs to pick up the players from hotels. I always allowed forty-five minutes to get from the hotel to the tennis center, another forty-five to get out to the practice court, thirty minutes of warm-up starting two hours before the match, then I ate again. For a 1pm match at the US Open, I scheduled the pick-up from my hotel for 9:30am.

The locker room thinned way out this late in the tournament. Instead of the few hundred players on day one, there were four men, four women, plus the doubles draw. Gerhardt was already there when I walked in. The top four players in the world were in the tightest cluster of tour ranking points in history. I was ranked four and if I beat Gerhardt and also went on to win the final, I'd be the new number one.

Ben Archer was ranked number three and in the other semifinal against the twenty-eighth seed who'd broken through. If Ben won the tournament, he'd take the number one spot.

Gerhardt stood and walked over to me with his hand out. "Good luck today, Anton. I hope we have a great match."

"Me too. Good luck."

"I'll miss you on the tour."

"I doubt for very long, but thanks."

"Maybe we can get a drink or lunch some time. I'd like to ask you how you've handled it all over the years."

That struck me as something I should have done when twenty-five. "Sure. Any time."

He nodded thanks and we walked to separate lockers, opponents again. You don't get to number one without being able to treat even a friend as a conquest.

I stayed in my cushioned chair and didn't think about the match but found that I couldn't help but wonder about Gerhardt. What road had he taken? His father, family, loves, books, steroids? Can his coach hand him a racket and get Pavlovian saliva in response? Is he up late at night in bed with eyelids squeezed shut and wondering when his masquerade will end? Does he love anyone? Has he learned how to love? Does he know anyone? Does he know himself?

Elite tennis players are soldiers who enlist at age eight rather than eighteen.

I'd had an early warm-up with Gabe on a practice court and my match time was in forty minutes. Ben Archer's match was after mine in probably five hours so it was unusual for him to be in the locker room so early, but in he walked.

Ben walked over to me looking unsure of himself. Everyone left a player alone right before a match. We always had to give a few words to the TV reporter on our way to the court which was a nuisance we tolerated. Otherwise, players were left alone but Ben wanted a moment.

I was seated far enough from Gerhardt that low tones wouldn't reach him. Ben said to me, "You got this guy."

"Thanks."

"I'm rooting for you. As always."

"It'd be fun to play you one more time," I said. "Fitting."

"Anyway," he said, embarrassed, "after all these years, and you leaving now, I just thought I ought to stop in and say a word. I'll leave you to it."

He turned and started walking out and I said, "Ben." He walked back to me so we were close and in low tones again and I said, "How the hell did you do it all this time? Make it all look so calm, intended. Easy."

"Me, make it look easy? I've been jealous of you my whole career. You're the flashier player. More talented, really. I'm just the plodder, the work horse. It never was easy for me."

I didn't think he understood what I meant. "That aside though. I don't mean the playing, the results. I mean the life. Did you find parts of it as lonely as I did? As miserable?"

He smiled. We'd never exchanged much more than greetings. Maybe some looks that expressed comradeship if you could read into them. But now I was being as frank with him as I'd ever been with anyone. He said, "My dad was a machine worker. He punched a clock and went out on the assembly plant floor for long shifts every day. So I've always treated this as a job, punching the clock. This is better than the assembly plant." He shrugged. "And what's more, my dad doesn't have to punch a clock anymore. But, yeah, it was lonely."

I nodded. "I hope we have one more match together."

I dressed and stretched and meditated until it was time to take the court. We walked from the locker room down the long familiar hallway to the stadium court, the hallway lined with large photographs of former champions, my photograph there among them, and I looked at the stranger in it.

At the end of the hallway was a reporter. I walked second and gave her a short comment about needing to play hard and respect

Gerhardt's game, and then there was Charlie, the security guard at the head of the tunnel, standing where he had always stood for the last ten years.

He never said a word in any of the matches of any prior years but that day he said, "Good luck, Anton." It felt like God choosing sides in a sporting event.

I stepped past Charlie to the open air and very white clouds that bring only shade. A cool day would favor me and my older legs.

We had yet to warm up and the match wouldn't start for another twenty minutes so the stadium was only about ten percent full. There was a legends box where former champions and tennis greats would sit for the match. A retiring former number one and an American brings them out. Agassi, Courier, Borg and Laver were there. Agassi usually didn't come to this stuff but we'd stayed in touch since I played his charity event. He nodded to me. Agassi never had the prettiest game, not a game like mine at all, but he was the player whose retirement I identified with the most.

I saw John McEnroe standing in the booth with a headset lowered around his neck. I hoped I'd have the kind of day that would have him saying good and hyperbolic things about me. Patrick wouldn't be there calling the match with him. He'd be down in a player's box as Gerhardt's coach.

I looked to my own player's box where Ana was just taking a seat next to my parents, Panos and Kristie, and Gabe. I smiled at how gorgeous Ana was, certain I'd never get used to it.

Gerhardt and I hit warm-up balls and I felt good, relaxed. My joints felt lubricated and strong. I'd taken everything Bobby gave me, maybe for the last time, and I was sure Gerhardt had taken something similar. He was an inch taller, twenty-five pounds heavier and all muscle.

The match started on Gerhardt's serve and he held for the first game. I then served well but Gerhardt returned great, jumping on even my best serves and he broke me easily. I broke his serve, then he broke me back.

I dropped all four of my service games in the first set, losing the set 6–2. I'd lost serve only twice in the tournament and now four times in the first set. Gerhardt had held his serve twice, then the only two games I took were off his serve.

The bizarre thing was that I was playing about my best. I was serving great but he was returning out of his mind.

Gerhardt held for the first game of the second set then we switched sides. I was rattled and needed the time in my chair. I was serving well, hitting my spots and still not winning. I needed to take more chances on my serve.

I stepped to the baseline to serve and decided to hit a flat hard serve up the middle. It was pure off my racket. I felt the gentle weight of the ball through my strings as I sent a meteor across the net that hit the T of the service box. A serve like that had never not been an ace for me but Gerhardt was already there, stepping into the court, shoulder turned, blocking a backhand return that came back so quickly that it skirted past my forehand side for a winner.

He'd guessed right. I couldn't have hit a better serve but if he committed to the right guess and sat on it, then the faster my serve the less time I'd have to get ready for the return.

My next serve to the ad court I decided to go wide. I slammed it high in the service box and it kicked up and wide but Gerhardt was there and he leaned into a backhand return for a winner up the line.

He looked up at me like a boxer who'd taken my best punch

and smiled back. My serve was my strength and I was serving my best and losing.

I hit two more serves that might have been aces on other days but Gerhardt took chances again, guessing right both times and he returned winners to take my service game at love.

I had to prepare to return Gerhardt's next service game but I was dazed. I couldn't understand what was happening to me on the court. Every time he guessed and he showed up early.

Then it occurred to me. Even that he was guessing on every one of his returns told me something. He wasn't a low-ranked qualifier taking chances against a top guy. He was number one. He ought to be playing straight up, especially if up love–40 on my serve.

That the four guesses were correct told me something more. I had a tell.

His team must have looked at tape of my serve and found a tell. Patrick Damn McEnroe. It had happened with other top players. Becker had a tell. He'd do something with his tongue that would tip the opponent what he planned to do with his serve. Amazing that in what could be my last match, my tell was out and used against me.

John McEnroe would be in the booth saying I was playing well, just up against a guy out to prove he was number one, but I had new optimism at my revelation, more energy in my steps between and during points.

Gerhardt served well and held in a tough game to go up 3–0 in the second set.

We switched sides again and I came to the baseline to serve. I shuffled my feet, twitched my mouth and tongue, darted my eyes side to side, repointed my shoulders and jerked my head side to side. I looked like I had a neurological disorder. Gerhardt was fascinated.

I tossed quickly and straight ahead. I always tossed to the same spot no matter where I served so I knew my toss wasn't the tell.

I was serving wide to his forehand and my ball was six inches out. I wasn't certain but I didn't think he had a jump on it. I decided to go for it on my second serve. What the hell, I'd lost my last service game at love so I might as well take a chance. I went through the same crazy routine then I tossed and plastered an ace down the middle.

Gerhardt's feet didn't move. At all.

The next serve Gerhardt guessed wrong and slipped trying to change direction. Another ace, an embarrassing one. Momentum shift. I was certain I wouldn't drop another service game in the match. I took the second set 6–3.

Mentally tough players can put a firewall between sets, like the *Titanic,* only better. But this was worse for Gerhardt. His huge knowledge advantage coming into the match had cost me only a set and now I'd evened that up. He wasn't even frustrated yet. He was still confused. His frustration would come when I creamed him.

I took the third set 6–2 and was up 4–1 in the fourth and what should have been the deciding set. I reached up to spin a second serve out wide to the ad court and my back went. I felt a sharp pain that seized me like an assassin garroting my lower back with piano wire.

Gerhardt managed a weak return of my serve but I couldn't move for his ball. Immediate injury timeout.

I moved to my chair on tiptoes trying not to antogonize my lower back. I sat as slowly as I could while a tournament trainer ran out to check me. He asked me how bad and I said very. He made the assessment for a full injury timeout back in the locker room so a trainer got under each of my arms and helped me off the court. We walked through the locker room to a small training room with padded table where I lay on my stomach.

Bobby was there. He prepared an injection, probably cortisone or something like it, while a trainer gently rubbed out my back.

Minutes passed. It didn't hurt if I didn't move but it was time to play or default. I stood and walked back out on my own, afraid of the pain but not feeling it right then. I paced along the baseline, keeping my back rod-straight and tried a slow service motion with my arm. No searing pain but I felt my back muscles were tired and tweaked like a torture victim's.

I had to finish out my service game and I thought about serving underhand. Instead I hit a flat-footed serve with no pop and Gerhardt ripped the return past me mercilessly. I lost that service game and went on to lose the fourth set 6–4.

It was an even game so there was no reprieve to me of switching ends and resting in my chair. I called a second injury timeout and shuffled to sit down. The trainer ran back out and this time I lay belly-down on the court by the chair and he rubbed out my back again. Humiliating, but it felt good.

With my cheek to the court I could see up into my player's box. My mother and father, to me now just fans that I used to know well, looked panicked. Panos and Kristie, holding hands, meeting my gaze. Ana had her hands to her face trying to wish away my pain.

I thought again about Joe Montana, knowing this might be the last time I could look up at a stadium crowd, feel the roar and then the hush, repeating like ocean waves.

The umpire called time. I pushed back to my knees then stood all the way. I was still scared of my back but it felt looser. Gerhardt looked eager to finish me, maybe a little frustrated with the timeout.

It was his serve and I decided to guess. He wouldn't serve into my body. I figured he'd serve wide and test my movement. He tossed and I cheated three steps to the right and sat on a forehand. I had guessed right and banged a winner up the line. The New York crowd roared for me and I felt their energy fuel me.

It can be tricky for a healthy player to face an injured player. The healthy player should just play his game but sometimes doesn't. Gerhardt threw in a double fault, then nerves started to grip him. It was visible to me. I broke his serve then risked more on my own serve and held to go up 2–0 in the fifth and final set.

If Gerhardt knew how badly I was hurt, he would have settled in, gotten down to business and finished me. But he didn't know and he couldn't settle down. His game got tight, his strokes shortened up and his decision making was erratic, taking chances at the wrong times, nerves making him try to end the points too soon.

Fans watching at home on TV can see for themselves when control of a match passes from one player to the other. Their observation is validated by McEnroe's commentary from the booth, then borne out on the court.

I had control of the match, the crowd noise for me almost loud enough to break the stadium, giving strength to me and taking it from Gerhardt.

With the external stimulation I thought I had enough to last and carry the set and match. I was certain McEnroe was saying that to all the televisions. I knew even if I did win, they'd have to carry me on the court for the final.

As the points played out, I grew more certain of winning. Gerhardt took some points but that made the crowd even crazier when

I took the next ones. I could see he didn't want to play anymore, wanted off the court, away from the stage. He had the "kill me quickly" look I had also known.

I won the match and shuffled back to the training room for relief.

46

I got slaughtered in the final. Ben Archer had won his semifinal so my slaughter was at his hands. Two days was not enough time for my back to recover much. I refused to retire from the match, especially to Ben whom I respected and who would take another major and the number one ranking with the win while I would take on a new life. He won 6–3, 6–1, 6–0.

The tournament officials had reserved the players' lounge for me after the awards ceremony so that I could linger privately and drink in the final moments of my professional tennis and I sat there with my family, my team and Ana.

My father and I had a long embrace and when we pushed back from each other still holding each other's shoulders at arm's length, there was a feeling of real parting with finality. I was retired now and released from his dreams. He had no plan for me after tennis, no vision or hopes for what I might be. I barely had that myself.

I hugged my mother who smiled and, despite her crying, looked happier and healthier than I'd ever seen her. She touched the side of my shoulder, turned me like a dance partner and led me a few steps from the others.

She said, "Anton, I hope now you will have time to be bored. And I look forward to seeing what you do about that."

This was meant to convey great meaning, be a triumphant moment, a truth shared between us and generations so powerful that we would shed tears of happiness. But what I felt was a dump truck grinding its gears with the sharp shriek of metal on metal as it raised its box bed to unload a great heap of guilt. She could unload it but I didn't have to pick it up. I could walk right past. "Thanks, Mom."

Kristie gave me a deep hug, lasting a moment longer than normal and that felt like family. Panos hugged me next and said, "Welcome to the real world." I was happy to be there. A Greek whose ship had sailed to port on Ellis Island for a new start.

Gabe, Bobby and Adam were subdued and sullen, talking more with my family than with me. They all had new jobs lined up except Adam. Gabe had taken up with a twenty-three-year-old American based out of Florida who was ranked fifty-five in the world. Bobby had taken on a few baseball clients. Adam was headed to Nicaragua for an indefinite surf trip.

My father was most comfortable engaging with Gabe, asking a few questions and offering a million opinions. He and I rarely spoke since his Wimbledon disruption and even more rarely made eye contact.

Ana gave my family space to be with me, not staying right at my side but moving among us, selflessly lending vitality where it was needed. She was the only one who was uncompromisingly with me and who knew me the way I knew me. What I wanted most was to be alone with her but that would come later and this time was important too. She understood that and gave me patience.

For an hour we stayed there drinking water and sipping champagne. There were toasts but no one was under the illusion this was a celebration. It was a farewell. I needed to get back home to lie down. Gabe, Bobby, Adam and I parted like battalion mates shipping back stateside who would return to their small towns and try to exchange Christmas cards each year.

I told my parents, Panos and Kristie that I'd see them very soon, then Ana and I left to be with each other.

We spent a day in Manhattan resting and packing, then drove to a house in East Hampton that Ana had rented for the month of September as my retirement present.

The first few mornings I woke early and walked the beach by myself, counting steps. I walked four thousand three hundred paces one day, twenty-one hundred the next. The counting required concentration that gave me a headache and drove off relaxation to a faraway place but I couldn't walk or be alone another way.

Then I'd stop to look over the water and think terrible thoughts. What did a specialized tool do when the job was done? Did they melt it down to use the material for something else, or did they just hang it on a picture hook for people to admire?

I thought about Paul Newman, a committed actor who evolved to be more than any one definition. He put his brand on things, not the other way around. Literally. Harder to do for an athlete, maybe, though Roger Staubach did it after quarterbacking the Cowboys. Staubach was the Paul Newman of sport, but how the hell did he do it?

By the second week I stopped counting steps and started walking more with Ana. She had hired a chef to come each day to cook lunch and dinner so we lived like honeymooners, lounging, talking, reading, exploring. I found more time with her was better. Even more would be even better.

In our third week we took a morning walk on the empty beach. We walked five minutes in silence as a happy complement to conversation. In the sky three planes left a skywriting contrail, weaving the lines among each other into a pattern. There is a spiritual nature to the number three. Father, Son and Holy Ghost. A trinity. Two can make a third.

I took Ana's hand and found myself on one knee looking up at her. She lifted her sunglasses above her forehead and looked back, amused, like I might recite Shakespeare.

I didn't have a plan, didn't have specific thoughts, I just had a feeling. Given a season to deconstruct the feeling into specific thoughts it would have been these: What matters most in our time on Earth is our relationships with others. My relationship with you is the only one that has ever been healthy, good, grounded in who I really am, the only one to make me happy, and I think I make you happy too. This relationship gives meaning to my life and I want to spend the rest of the time that I have nurturing us, above all else.

From my knee I said, "Ana, will you marry me?"

Right away it was clear she did not expect this. She looked no longer at me but through me while her mind saw images of me and us and she worked through life questions in flashes of possibilities, evaluating. There would be no specific thoughts for her either, just the feeling conjured within seconds.

But the seconds ticked by, like a player bouncing the ball before the service toss. Each second landed with a thud in my ears while I looked at her and she looked through me, her head at a slight angle as though I might have been only an apparition and not real.

I had moved prematurely in the craze of my love and retirement, and in our time together now she would be unnatural, like a cornered animal retreating from a curious and hungry aggressor. So I feared.

It was a diabolic ten seconds before she recovered from the stun. Then through her rush of feeling she arrived at the answer that made her eyes smile moments before the smile spread to her mouth. "Yes."

I was a frontiersman again. This time I was in love, and this time my life was mine.

ACKNOWLEDGEMENTS

One of the few constants in my young writing career has been my terrific agents, Lane Zachary and Todd Shuster. They have guided me through the process three times now, and Lane worked with me on several drafts of this novel. I appreciate their advice and friendship.

My editor, George Witte, and I shared a vision for this book and he had excellent suggestions. I've had a range of experience with editors, and it's my hope to work with George on many books to come.

Thanks also to the rest of the team at Macmillan/St. Martin's Press: Don Weisberg, Sally Richardson, Dori Weintraub, Laura Clark, Sara Thwaite, Alastair Hayes. Thanks to Kathleen Carter Zrelak.

In the course of my research for this novel, I spoke with several friends and athletes who provided valuable input: James Blake,

John Isner, Tiago Espirito Santo, Wayne Street, Sara Whalen Hess, Scott Kegler, Andy Postman.

Many thanks to Jean Frazier, Anna Serbek, Eileen Mitchell and MaryEllen Kazar at the Beach Haven Library. My favorite place to write.

My mother and father introduced to me both (fun and recreational) tennis and a love of reading. An important combination for this book. I still exchange book recommendations with my mom and am always fascinated to hear her insightful take.

Yates, Yardley and Thatcher attended my last Barnes & Noble book signing, though they did cartwheels around the audience rather than listen in. They've come to know the libraries and bookstores as my offices as well as a place to find books for themselves. Their interest in reading is growing. Each day that I write, in the back of my mind is the thought that one day they will turn these pages too. One more reason to write my best.

Last and most, thank you to Megyn. She is with me from inception to completion and is the first, often the only, person I want to share with, in any aspect of my writing or of my life. Our love grows stronger.